Polly Peartree and the Great Wolfwich Mystery

Lee A. Smith

1

I always thought I was a normal kid. It wasn't until I moved to the mysterious little town of Wolfwich that I realised that there is no such thing as a normal kid.

I guess it all started at the start of the summer holidays when my parents delivered some pretty shocking news.

* * *

"What!" I exclaimed, spraying my sugar coated cereal from my mouth in the process. My mum repeated the bombshell in the same, stern motherly tone. My mum was quite short, slim and had long brown hair and a freckly face. Her hair was long and straight and silky, unlike my own which was a mess even when brushed. She wore a thick blue jumper even though the weather outside was warm and very summery indeed.

"We're moving house on Monday," Mum repeated, looking at me intently to see my reaction.

"Tomorrow?" I enquired. "But school has only just finished for the year, I can't start my school holidays moving house. We better not be moving far, what about Sara and Naz?" I took a breath as I blurted all this out in one quick outburst.

Sara and Naseera were identical twins and my best mates from school; ever since primary school and that was five years ago. We were hardly ever apart when we weren't at home, and the thought of moving house somewhere away from them was unspeakable. I began to pick at the sleeve of my favourite blue checked shirt, which was my favourite of many checked shirts of varying colours. They went well with the blue jeans I always wore that covered my knobbly knees. Picking at my sleeves was a sure sign that I was getting annoyed or frustrated and I think my dad noticed it.

"It's a nice little town called Wolfwich," my dad chipped in. He had been eating his egg on toast quietly until now, but decided to say something.

Wolfwich? I thought, my mind still in a daze from the bombshell. *What sort of name is Wolfwich?*

"You will make plenty of new friends I'm sure," Mum said and gave a motherly smile that I'm sure only mums know how to do. *They must give parents training to give answers like that,* I thought bitterly.

"But I don't want new friends, Mum. I have friends."

Doesn't she know that eleven year old kids don't want to be moving home in the summer holidays to make new friends? "And where is Wolfwich exactly?" I asked. It was certainly nowhere that I had ever heard of before.

"It's a little town to the north of here. We get to go on a nice long journey in the car to get there," my dad said. His grey moustache wiggled when he spoke, as did his glasses. With his wild, bushy hair, now going a little bit grey, he always reminded me of a little terrier. A terrier with glasses, of course. He was wearing a white shirt and black trousers. He always wore a white shirt. I don't know if this was because he worked from home and wanted to have a smart appearance at all times or he just liked wearing white shirts.

"But why are we moving?" I almost whined; I was beginning to feel upset. This wasn't how I wanted to start my six weeks holiday.

"Polly," my mum said, for that was my name (my full name is Polly Patricia Peartree, which I always think is quite cool). "It's just something we have to do, which I hope you will understand soon enough."

That seemed like another parent answer that wasn't supposed to make any sense. I gave the best sulky look I could muster, which was a pretty good sulky look, considering how upset I was.

"I really don't wanna go," was all I could think of to say. Mum, who had been sat opposite me at the kitchen table, got up and walked round to give me a cuddle.

"You'll enjoy it Polly, I promise. It will be quite an adventure." She gave me a big squeeze, which cheered me up a little. "It won't be the last time you see your friends. In fact, why don't you go round to see Naseera and Sara? I'll ring their mum and I can arrange a sleepover for tonight?" Mum smiled and winked at me. I gave into her charms as I usually always do.

"Okay Mum, but I'm really gonna miss this place."

I couldn't believe I was giving in to this decision so easily, but what else could I do? I just hoped the twins wouldn't be as upset as I was feeling, or worse; I really hoped they weren't angry at me.

"We all will miss it sweetie," Mum replied, "but

like I said, this will be the start of quite an adventure!"

2

Half an hour later, I had packed a small rucksack with all the essentials for a sleepover (nightgown, collection of music, my Amaze-All-Portable-Science experiment kit – more about this later, I promise) and the unessential things which parents always want you to pack (toothbrush, socks, a sandwich) and I was running round the street corner heading towards my two best friends' house. As I got around the corner, who should I run into, quite literally because we both ended up in a heap on the floor, but Sara, followed a second later by Naz!

"We have some terrible news!" Exclaimed the twins together as we finally untangled ourselves and got up from the floor. The twins had the longest, thickest, darkest black hair I had seen on any girls, so untangling ourselves really was quite a task. The twins both wore identical long skirts and identical blue blouses. In fact, the only way I could generally tell them apart was because Sara had a small birthmark on her nose, and Naz squinted a lot as though she needed to wear glasses. I often told her that it would make them easier to tell apart if she *did* wear glasses.

"Me too, I'm afraid," I said. "But I think mine may be worst news so I shall let you go first."

The twins didn't waste any time in delivering their news, barely sharing a glance before blurting it out, "We're moving house!" Sara shouted.

"On Monday!" Naz shouted a fraction of a second later.

"You just stole my news!" I exclaimed, my head suddenly felt all fuzzy and I didn't know what else to say.

"What!" The twins cried out together.

"I'm moving on Monday too, my parents just told me over breakfast."

The twins stared at each other and then back at me. Naz squinted at me and Sara rubbed unconsciously at the mark on her nose.

"Ours too, my Choc Flakes went everywhere!" That was Sara; what Naz said next really did make my head feel fuzzy and I had to sit down on the nearest garden wall.

"A little town called Wolfwich," was what Naz said.

"There's something strange going on here," I said with my hands holding my head. "That's where we are moving, too!"

After the initial shock of this unusual news, we decided a plan of action was required. We were good at making plans and in ten minutes we were gathered in the local park, sat on the swings. This was our regular "Command Centre" for when emergency plans were needed. The first plan of action was to contact all our friends and school contacts on Sara's mobile phone to find out whether anyone else was suddenly moving home. Sara loved her phone and was always playing annoying games on it, or finding even more annoying ringtones for it. Naz felt she didn't need her own phone as she and her sister were never apart. This contact list consisted of Becky Summers, Julie Saunders and the only boy any of us knew – Roger Robbins.

The results were disappointing. Naz's theory of all the kids from our school being relocated for some mysterious reasons the adults were keeping to themselves seemed to be unfounded. Our three other friends weren't going anywhere.

"So plan 2 is surveillance," Naz announced as she swung ever higher on the swing. "Stealth and ingenuity will be required. We must be invisible as we try and find out what our parents are planning."

Naz was our chief planner and she got into the role with great enthusiasm.

"The sleepover our parents tried to plan must be cancelled as we need to keep an eye on your parents too, Polly."

I nodded. We needed to get to the bottom of this and Naz meant business. "You don't have a mobile so you will need to use the house phone once every hour for regular updates. Remember stealth is key, so we are going to need code-words. Any ideas?"

The ideas flowed as we swung higher and higher. I headed back home twenty minutes later with my head buzzing, nervous at the prospect of spying on my parents and wondering if anything sinister really was going on. Operation "Parentspy" was ready to commence.

3

Mum was watching television when I returned home and Dad was making something or other in his shed. My excuse for returning — Sara had suddenly started feeling ill and I didn't want to catch anything — was accepted without question.

I decided I would pretend to read as I awaited Naz's first call, and kept an eye on my mum, in the hope she would do anything out of the ordinary. I soon realised my mum was very boring. She didn't leave her armchair for two hours and was laughing at the most unfunny television programmes. When the phone did ring I dived up energetically.

"I'll get it!" I yelled before my mum had even registered that the phone was ringing.

"Hello?" I asked cautiously.

"Naz here," the voice on the other end whispered. Naz calling meant that no important information had been gathered. Had it been Sara, then that meant something had been discovered worth reporting.

"All's well, Naz," I declared loudly so Mum knew the call was for me. This also told Naz that nothing had been discovered on my end. Had there been something worth telling I would have said, "What's happening?" It had all been well thought out in my opinion and it made me feel like a secret agent passing on important military information.

"My parents are so boring," whispered Naz.

"Haven't left the television all day so far."

"Yeah, mine too." I glanced at my mum at the far side of the room. She didn't appear to be listening to me but I lowered my voice anyway, just in case. "Mum is laughing at rubbish programmes. I might focus my attention on Dad in his shed."

"Good plan, Polly. You may need to try out stage two."

Stage two was my idea and was where the stealth and sneakiness came into action. Before I could reply, Naz butted in suddenly, "Gotta go Pol. Mum just got up from the sofa!" She hung up and I returned to the book I wasn't really reading.

My rucksack that I had took with me earlier was at the side of the armchair I was sat in and was still packed. I reached inside the bag and pulled out my Amaze-All-Portable-Science experiment kit. Inside here, amongst several test tubes, bottles, powders, batteries and other assorted science bits and bobs was what I was looking for. It was my portable voice recorder. This was meant for recording important scientific experiments but today it was going to have another purpose. Mum was still focussed on the television so I got up and switched the voice recorder on and walked with it hidden up my unbuttoned shirt sleeve. This was stage two: secret voice recording was ready to commence.

"Going to see what Daddy is up to, Mum," I announced, and she waved her hand in acknowledgement. It appeared as though nothing was going to disturb her while her favourite programme was still on.

"Let's see what this produces," I said under my breath. I reached up my sleeve for the recorder then pressed the record button. There was a bookshelf just below the telephone and I placed the recorder carefully and well hidden behind one of the books, then left the room.

My dad was an inventor. He worked for a big electronics company in town, creating items that helped the company's products go faster, last longer or do things that other company's similar products could not do. It was apparently a very well paid job, although his office must have been based in his shed as he barely left it apart from meals and bedtime.

I knocked on the shed door and entered cautiously. It was always advised to enter the shed cautiously as there were often explosions as experiments or ideas went wrong.

"Hi, Dad!" I exclaimed after peeping round the door and seeing that he was sat drinking a cup of tea and not dealing with anything dangerous or fragile, as was often the case.

"Hi sweetie. I thought you were with the twins?"

I went through my little white lie once again. I felt more uncomfortable lying to my dad then my mum; I have been told often I was always a daddy's girl.

"Daddy?" My tone suggested I was going to ask something important. I decided there and then that my stealth approach wouldn't work on my dad so I would just talk to him instead.

"Yes, Polly?" He put down his large mug of tea,

looking concerned. "Is this about moving house?"

"Yes, Dad," I replied, wondering how to begin my chat. I looked around the cramped shed, which was dominated by a large wooden bench piled high with electronic equipment and tools, and thought of something to say. "If we are moving on Monday won't you lose your job?"

"You know I work from my shed Pol. I could work anywhere in the world if I wanted to."

"But you couldn't take your shed with you, Dad."

"No, but I can take everything in it with us. Where we are going I will have a huge cellar all to myself, much more room than this cramped space."

I decided to test my dad and check his reaction. "I'm really going to miss Sara and Naz, Daddy. I won't get to see them every day."

My dad smiled, and was that a little knowing glint in his eye or did I imagine it?

"They really won't be that far away sweetheart," he answered cryptically then stood up suddenly. "Oh, ham and jam!" He exclaimed. This was something of a favourite phrase of his when something went wrong or he remembered something urgent. "I need to make an urgent report with work, you don't mind going back indoors do you, Polly?"

"Of course not, Dad."

I left him then and though I wasn't certain, I had made my opinion; my parents knew that the twins were also moving, and they were keeping something secret.

4

My opinion was confirmed when I managed to get my recorder back and had time to listen to it in the quiet and privacy of my bedroom. This was a few hours after my meeting with Dad. Having just finished a big tea of egg and chips and beans, I managed to sneak the recorder out of the bookshelf and excused myself. The recorder needed charging and I just hoped there was something worth listening to before it had cut out.

After I had charged the recorder for a while, I pressed the playback button and listened nervously. For two minutes there was nothing apart from background noise and the occasional burst of laughter from my mum. Then I heard a familiar theme tune as my mum's favourite show ended, then, a few seconds later, the sound of the telephone receiver being picked up.

Yes! I thought. *This is what I have been waiting for.*

I couldn't hear the dialling tone, but I could hear my mum's nails tapping on the bookshelf as she waited, and then she spoke.

"Hi Anita. It's me, Jean."

Anita. That was Sara and Naz's mum. She was a designer and had designed the identical skirts the twins wore. I held my breath in excitement. I couldn't hear what was said on the other end of the conversation, but I heard my mum's reply clearly:

"Yeah, I'm good thanks. Did you catch the end of

Barley Street? I can't believe Janice ran off with Frank!"

Oh great, I thought as I listened. *A call about boring TV shows again. This is well worth my attention.* I continued to listen however, and soon the subject changed. I could only hear Mum's half of the conversation but it soon became intriguing.

"How are the twins? How did they take the news?" … "I would have thought they would have told each other too, but Polly hasn't said a thing." … "Let's hope the questions don't start too soon, eh?" … "That's one thing they won't like, Anita." … "Let's hope the boards are strong enough this time. I've heard nasty tales of others getting loose and running wild before they are ready." … "They will be fine Anita, and Polly will be fine with it when she finds out." … "It's never easy being a …"

The recording switched itself off here, just when I thought it was getting very, very interesting. Several phrases from the conversation twirled around my head especially the bit about something *"getting loose and running wild"*. I wondered too what the word I missed right at the end might have been. There was one thing that I did know however, and that was that I needed to talk to the twins urgently. Neither of them had stuck to the original plan of calling every hour and I wondered if they had caught the other end of the conversation I had listened to. I hoped that they had; I had a feeling that their mum's end of the conversation was a lot more revealing than at this end. There was only one thing for it – an emergency meeting. It was only 5 in the afternoon, so I stuffed my recorder into my jeans pocket and jogged downstairs. Mum was standing in the landing surrounded by a mountain of empty cardboard boxes.

"Ah, Polly! Are you here to help me pack? Lots to do and little time to do it in!"

"Er, Mum?" I gave her my best pleading look which she knew meant I was going to ask her for something.

"What is it dear?"

"I was hoping to go outside for a bit to the park. It is likely my last ever chance to go down to the park what with us moving tomorrow and everything."

Mum considered this and I was sure she was going to say no. There seemed to be an awful lot of packing to get done and I would probably have to spend till midnight just sorting out my own cluttered room.

"Well, if you promise to be back by seven, then okay. Have you got your watch on?"

"Thanks Mum!" I exclaimed as I lifted the sleeve of my shirt to show her the bulky digital watch I liked to wear, then darted out of the house.

Phase one in arranging an emergency meeting was to get in touch with the twins without their parents' knowledge. This was arranged through the good old fashioned, but generally quite effective method of throwing a stone against their bedroom window. The twins' bedroom window was at the side of their large house, and conveniently a large tree was in their garden to keep me hidden. The stones where in plentiful supply from the gravel driveway and even with my bad aim it only took three stones for me to finally hit the window. There was no reply, so I waited a couple of minutes before trying again. They could be in any room of the house, so I was trusting a lot to luck. The second attempt proved that my luck was in, as Sara's face appeared at the window and I emerged out of hiding from behind the tree trunk to wave at her. She waved back and then Naz appeared at the window too.

I put my hands out in front of me and clenched them and rocked back and forth on my toes – my mime for swing. I voiced the words, *"Emergency meeting at the park,"* slowly. There was a pair of thumbs up and the twin faces disappeared. It was now a waiting game to see whether the twins could get out of the house and meet me at the park.

The swings were occupied by some young kids and their parents when I got there, so I sat on the roundabout instead. It was fifteen minutes later when Naz and Sara ran into the park to join me, their faces looking hot from the run.

"We couldn't call, Pol. We got roped into packing," Sara exclaimed.

"We can only chat for half an hour, then more packing," said Naz gloomily.

"It's alright gals. I have some news. My mum rang your mum."

I related the events of the day and replayed the recording. Frustratingly, they hadn't heard their mum on the phone due to being made to pack their bedroom, so they couldn't help with filling in the blanks, but, like myself, they still had plenty of questions.

"Who's getting loose?" Said Naz.

"Is someone getting locked up?" Asked Sara a fraction of a second later.

"What is it that we are going to find out?"

"And what is it not easy being?"

We couldn't answer any of the questions and we sat on the roundabout pushing it around with our feet as we thought.

"Replay that last sentence again Pol," said Sara suddenly. I did as she said and we listened once more to my mum's calming voice. "Polly will be fine with it when she finds out," a pause of a few seconds and then, "It's never easy being a ..."

"Hmm," Sara looked thoughtful. "You can almost hear the start of the next word, sort of an *oooh* sound."

"Oooh," repeated Naz. I replayed the last few words again and Sara was right: there was the slightest hint of another sound.

"*Ooowa Ooowa,*" said Sara repeatedly. "I think that the word begins with W, whatever it is."

I replayed the recording a final time and I had to agree with Sara. Now that she said it, there was definitely the start of a "W" word.

"It's never easy being a weirdo," said Naz and laughed.

"Walrus," I said, trying to be funny.

"Witch?" Sara suggested. Naz and I laughed and tried to think of more words that might fit. Sara had gone quiet again as though in deep thought. "We're moving to a place called Wolfwich. Wolf-witch. Think it could be a coincidence?"

"Don't be daft, Sara. There aren't any witches in real life," said Naz, but she didn't sound very confident. "What do you think, Pol?"

I didn't know what to think regarding witches. It sounded a bit far-fetched to me. But the whole day seemed to be heading in a very far-fetched direction.

"I'm not sure Naz, but I think we need to make a decision quickly before we head off back home. If we *do* head off back home that is."

"What do you mean?" Asked the twins in unison.

"I mean do we go with our parents and see what mysterious plans they have in store for us, or do we stay here. We could always run away?"

The twins looked at each other in horror at this idea and I knew that it was as daft an idea as it sounded in my head.

"Where would we run away to, Pol?" Sara asked.

It was a daft idea and I knew it. And also, I was far too intrigued about what our parents were keeping secret from us to even really consider running away. "Yeah I know, stupid idea!" I admitted and blushed.

"We are heading to this new place together, so whatever it is we will be facing, we can face it together," said Naz philosophically.

"Together forever," said Sara.

"Together forever," I repeated, and we left our local park for what was to be the last time.

5

I got home at quarter to seven and to my surprise the packing in the entire house had been completed!

"How on Earth?" I asked as I walked amongst the stacked boxes that filled the landing and what was once the living room.

"Oh, hi Pol," said Dad as he walked in from the kitchen with a glass of water. "We got through quite a bit while you were gone."

I looked at the stacked boxes in disbelief. This was more than just quite a bit, this was an entire house packed neatly into boxes. "But you had hardly started packing less than two hours ago, you and Mum can't have done all this in that time!"

"We find that there is time for anything, for those who work hard to make the time work for them," Dad stated mysteriously and chuckled to himself. He said strange things like that occasionally, and spent far too much time chuckling to himself in my opinion.

Was this another mystery or were my parents just very, very organised when it came to packing? My parents were usually so laid back, and Dad in particular was so messy that this neat pile of boxes only added to my confusion. They must have got the neighbours in to help; it was the only logical explanation. I was trying to make mysteries out of everything today, it seemed.

I re-ran what my dad had just said through my head and frowned.

"That makes no sense Daddy. Where are we going to sleep tonight anyway?"

It turned out that the sleeping bags and pillows where not yet packed and there was a nice cosy clearing amongst the boxes in which we could spend our final night in the house I had always called home.

By eleven the following morning, the town I had lived in all my life was a blur on the horizon as we sped along the motorway towards our mysterious destination in the small blue family car. The vast majority of our belongings had travelled ahead of us, very early in the morning, in a large removal truck belonging to one of my Dad's best friends, who was called Terry. Terry had brought his son along with him for the journey. His name was Jamie and he was a very pale and quiet boy a year younger than me. I recognised him from school although I had never spoke to him.

"Well I guess the adventure starts here!" Declared Dad excitedly as he tapped the steering wheel in time to one of the latest pop tunes on the radio.

"Yeah, Dad," I said distractedly. I was tired after getting up at half past four to help load the truck, and I was also thinking of the twins. Were they behind us somewhere or had they already set off? I kept turning back and looking at the sea of traffic all around us, hoping to see the big green people-carrier that belonged to Sara and Naz's dad.

My mum, who was sat next to me in the back seat patted my knee. "I can see you're missing our old home already, sweetie. We have some good news to share with you if you want, haven't we Alf?"

"Yeah, I think we can let her know," said Dad. I think I knew what they were going to announce but I turned back to face my parents with interest.

"Really, what is it Dad?"

"Well, Polly. You will be seeing the twins a lot sooner than you might think. They will be moving to Wolfwich too!"

Mum smiled and Dad chuckled, looking up at me through his rear-view mirror. I felt relieved that my parents had not kept this secret from me for long; perhaps they weren't planning anything sinister after all! For a split second I was torn between acting surprised at this news and telling the truth that I already knew. I decided on the truth.

"I know that, Dad. They told me yesterday."

Mum smiled. It seemed she suspected that I knew all along. I hoped she didn't also have any idea about our secret surveillance plans from yesterday too.

"Why are they moving too, Mum? It seems very strange to us."

There was quite a long pause before anyone answered and it was my dad who broke the silence. "We can't go into details just yet Polly, but it will all make sense in a little while, okay?"

Another mysterious answer, but I hoped they were correct and that things would start to make sense soon.

"I can't wait to see them. Will it be tonight? Will they be living nearby? Can I ring them up? How big is the town?"

When I get excited I like to ask lots of questions at once.

There was another long pause. I got the feeling there was still an awful lot of secrets being kept from me. Mum answered this time.

"You might not be able to see them for at least a few days, Pol. There are a few things going on we can't discuss just yet. There aren't any phone signals in Wolfwich at the moment either, I'm afraid. But as to your other question, it is a rather small town, quite a small, friendly community actually."

No phone signal? What sort of town was this anyway not having a phone signal? Sara wasn't going to be happy with that. She loved her phone and was always ringing my house-phone whenever she had the opportunity. There were so many other questions I wanted to ask then but didn't, chief amongst these being, just what was going on that they couldn't discuss?

Instead, I said, "Okay Mummy," meekly, then sat quietly looking out of the window. I wondered if my two best friends knew anything more than me at this moment what awaited for them in the increasingly mysterious little town of Wolfwich. I wondered if they had been told about the lack of a phone signal and how Sara especially had reacted to this.

It was about another twenty minutes before anyone spoke again and it was my mum asking if I would like a drink. She reached into a small rucksack and pulled out a large plastic bottle of what looked like my favourite summer fruit cordial.

"Yes please," I said as I took the offered bottle. I

drank thirstily - it seemed to be the first thing I had drank since waking up - then returned to the entertainment the view from the car window offered. The clouds above me, and the cars in front of me, and the hedges, and fields beyond this blurred into one greeny-purple colour as our car sped along the motorway. I felt myself getting drowsy, and in no time at all I was sound asleep, slumped against my mother's shoulder.

6

I must have been asleep for a long time, for the sky was no longer blue, but pink. The sun was nothing but a reddish-orange glow on the horizon, and looking at my watch told me it was seven o' clock. We were no longer on a busy motorway but driving slowly along a quiet and deserted country road.

"You had a nice long kip there, kid," my dad said. "We are almost there now."

I looked out the window at the shadowy surroundings and wondered how far we had travelled today. All I could see were large grassy hills and the occasional large house silhouetted against the fading sunlight.

"We are approaching the outskirts of the town now, you should see a sign coming up any moment."

That was Mum. She was pointing ahead between the two front seats, and sure enough, we were approaching a large sign on the side of the road. It appeared to be a painted sign with a picture of a large green hill and a pale sun above it. Below the hill was a welcome message:

Welcome to Wolfwich. The town where everyone can be themselves.

"What a strange slogan," I said as we passed the sign and officially entered the town of Wolfwich.

"Yes," said Dad. "It is a friendly community here."

We were driving along the small road for a further two minutes before I saw any sign of the town we had supposedly arrived at. The car turned a tight corner and we suddenly seemed to be very high up. The road had took us to a wide valley which we found ourselves at the top of, and below us the town was spread out and lit brightly like a star-lit sky. It was more like a large village than a town. There appeared to be only four or five main roads criss-crossing the valley and the lights from the houses suggested there was probably only a couple of hundred buildings down there. I looked across to the far side of the valley and gasped.

"Look Mum, there's two castles over there!"

There was indeed two large magnificent looking old castles, each one standing boldly atop of separate hills at the far end of the valley. The fading sunset gave both castles magnificent shadows that stretched down both hills.

"There's some very old families that live here, Pol," said my dad as he manoeuvred the car slowly down the winding road towards the centre of Wolfwich. "Very old and noble families that have lived in those castles for centuries."

"Cool!" I was impressed. The town was starting to look a little more interesting already.

"Legend has it that the two families are sworn enemies and they won't be seen in the same room together," my mum whispered to grab my attention. "They are quite reclusive so you may not see them at all for a good while."

"Who are they?" I asked, intrigued.

"The castle on the left belongs to an old Irish family. The O' Neill's. The one to the right belongs to the Marten's. Viktor Marten was an old pal of your father's, I believe."

My dad laughed at this. "We got into quite a bit of mischief back in our school days. Those were the days," he said, chuckling to himself once again.

I was going to ask Dad more about the mischief he got up to when I made a sudden connection – something that seemed like it could be important. "You went to school here in Wolfwich, Dad?"

Dad hesitated before he answered, looking up at his wife. "Well, I lived here for a while when I was your age, as did Mum, Polly. We never went to school here, but we sure learnt an awful lot. Just like you will."

My parents both lived here in Wolfwich at my age? Was this a key part to the mystery of moving here, or just coincidence? I decided to follow a hunch that had just occurred to me.

"And did Mr and Mrs Ahmed go to school here too?" I asked. They were the twins' parents. I felt like I could be getting somewhere in solving part of the mystery of our sudden move.

"You could be a detective, Polly!" My dad exclaimed as he laughed again. "Yeah they lived here too. Both a couple of years older than me though."

I had a lot more questions to ask but my dad changed the subject suddenly.

"Anyway, Pol. We have reached the bottom of the valley now. We will be at our new home in a minute."

"Really?" I asked excitedly, forgetting for a little while about questioning my dad further.

I looked around as we drove slowly down a cobbled street, trying to guess which house may be our new home. All the houses we passed were big stone detached houses with very large gardens both front and back. I spotted something very familiar a couple of hundred yards ahead of us. It was the large truck that had brought with it all of our belongings. We had finally arrived at our new home.

7

Inside our new house was very much like the last night in the old one – boxes stacked everywhere. But this house was much bigger. I had already decided on my new bedroom – a large room with painted blue walls and a large window with a view of the house next door and the rest of the street leading off to what I guessed was the centre of the town. More importantly to me, it offered a view in the distance of the two castles – either side of next door's chimney. There was all sorts of banging going on downstairs, so I was stood in my room now, trying to find some silence but failing, with a heavy box of some of my belongings in my hands. I stopped what I was doing once again and placed the box on the floor to take another look out of the window. I looked at both of the castles in turn. They were silhouetted against the last of the sunset, two dark shadows in the dusky sky.

"Perhaps no one lives there anymore," I said to myself.

A loud bang from downstairs was followed by my dad shouting his familiar curse.

"Oh, ham and jam!"

I think that was the third box he must have dropped since the unpacking began. I wondered again how they had managed to pack all this stuff so quickly and precisely when it seemed so much hard work unpacking.

"Guess I should go back down for another box," I sighed. Before I got out of my bedroom door, however, I heard heavy footsteps coming up the stairs. With the house being empty and unfurnished, every noise seemed to be magnified, and it sounded as though an elephant was thudding up the steps. It wasn't my mum or dad as I was expecting, but a little, pale, ten year old boy who stopped, panting, in front of me.

"Jamie!" I exclaimed, as I recognised the son of the removal truck's driver. "I thought you and your dad would have gone home by now?" I asked.

It was after nine at night by now and I had assumed Terry, his son, and the empty truck would have been heading on the long trip back south. I had saw the truck drive off an hour or so ago, a bright green truck with a big smily face on the side, and the slogan, *"Happy Man Deliveries – No Job Too Small!"*

Jamie had got his breath back, and he said in one quick outburst, "We have been home and unpacked our stuff and now Dad has said I can come to help you too and I thought I would say hi!"

It took me a few seconds to process and unravel what Jamie said. "Er, hi. Did you say unpack?"

"Yeah, we finished ages ago. I can't wait to go exploring tomorrow, what about you?"

"You don't mean to say you are moving here too?" I asked. Here was another strange development brewing in front of me. Another one of my parent's friends and their child had moved to this small town on the same night. I wondered yet again whether Sara and Naz had arrived in town and whether they had unravelled any of the mystery that we had been puzzling over since yesterday morning.

"Yeah, we are neighbours Polly!" Jamie laughed at this and ran past me into my bedroom. "Nice room! That's my house there!" Jamie was pointing out of the window at the nearest house, just a stone's throw away, separated only by an avenue of grass on either side of a paved garden path.

"Do you find it strange that we are both moving to this town on the same day?" I asked Jamie as we both looked out at his new house.

Jamie paused to consider this then said, "I guess so. I only found out on Saturday."

"I only found out yesterday. My best friends are both moving here today too. I haven't heard from them yet though."

We looked at each other nervously. It seemed that Jamie must have had the same idea in his head as me, because he said a few seconds later, "I think we may need to do some snooping around tomorrow. There seems to be something strange going on here."

"I completely agree, Jamie. Don't ask me why, but I think it might have something to do with those castles up there."

I pointed out the window to the distant shapes on the horizon. With more clouds in the sky now, the moon was obscured and the sky darker. It was harder to see the castles, but they still seemed to loom over the entire town.

"Dad told me that one of them is haunted. I forget which one," Jamie stated nervously.

"My dad said an old friend of his lived in the castle there on the right. I think he would have said if that one was haunted."

"I don't think my dad will let me go up there. What about yours?"

I was still looking out of the window at that moment and something unusual caught my eye. The removal truck that had been parked outside our house was driving slowly away up the street. It had drove away earlier, which was why I had assumed Jamie and his dad had left. It was definitely the same truck. The smily face on the side was hard to miss, even in the gloom. Yet here it was again, driving slowly down the road.

"Talking of your dad, do you know where he is going at this time?" I asked Jamie, pointing to the removal truck. He looked just in time to see the back end of the green vehicle disappear from sight up the road.

"The truck is meant to be in storage," Jamie answered. "Dad said he gave the keys to someone ages ago and he told me it was going in storage till we had settled in."

"Weird," I said out loud.

"Yeah, maybe there is no storage here," Jamie pondered. "It won't be Dad driving anyway, he was in his pyjamas when I popped over here to help. He told me not to be too long."

Was this yet another mysterious event, or just someone driving around looking for a place to store a large truck in a small town?

Thinking of removal trucks, it occurred to me then that the twins probably needed a truck to move all of their belongings here too.

"I don't suppose your dad had two trucks, did he?"

I could remember the number plate of the truck that brought all of our belongings – TEZ 51 – but it was too dark to notice the number plate on the truck that had just passed.

"No. The business isn't busy enough for two trucks. I don't think there will be much business in this small town either," Jamie answered gloomily.

"Ah," I replied, disappointedly. "I was thinking perhaps that truck that passed had my friends' belongings in. Surely they must have arrived hours ago."

"Would they be twins by any chance?" Jamie asked and I stared at him in disbelief.

"Yeah, Sara and Naz, how did you know?"

"Oh, we picked their stuff up after packing yours and our own, all three family's stuff! My dad's truck is the best!"

"You saw the twins?" I asked.

"No, the family had already left. Their house was empty when we loaded the stuff in. Dad was telling me all about Mr Ahmed being an old school friend and how he has two twin daughters who go to my school. He was telling me about your dad too, and about you going to my school too! I probably saw you and them together at school but I really don't remember."

Something occurred to me then. Jamie had been with his dad when they delivered the twins' belongings to their new home so he might be able to help me locate it! I asked Jamie this but he shook his head.

"I was fast asleep when we arrived. When I woke up, Dad was already here unloading our stuff next door."

"Ham and jam!" I said disappointedly, not even realising I had just stole my dad's favourite phrase. From the sound of it, Naz and Sara would have arrived here in Wolfwich way earlier than we had done, and I wondered again what they were up to at this moment.

They are probably resting after a long day of unpacking, I thought and then yawned. *Stop making mysteries out of nothing just because a truck has drove past a couple of times.*

I giggled to myself, mainly out of tiredness, and Jamie giggled too.

"Let's forget about the darn truck! I think that tomorrow I will find my friends, Naz and Sara, and then maybe we can have a closer look at those castles and see if they really are haunted. You can come along too if you want?"

Although he looked at me wide-eyed and almost terrified, Jamie said he would come along too. We both agreed we wouldn't mention anything about this to our parents, and so, after talking through a quick plan of action for tomorrow, Jamie returned to his new home next door, under a blaze of bright moonlight, and I went downstairs to continue with the unpacking.

8

"I'm sorry, Polly, but Sara and Naz won't be able to go out and explore today."

It was the morning after a long night of unpacking and I was sat with my parents round the breakfast table. My mum had just given me the first setback of the plan of action Jamie and I had decided upon yesterday.

"Why not, Mum?" I asked, trying not to sound disappointed, but I had a feeling my face betrayed me there. My hands were twiddling with my sleeves and I forced them to my sides, trying not to look anxious.

"They will still be busy getting settled in, Polly. We still have a lot to do, too."

"Can I at least know where they have moved to, Mum? I could help them unpack or something?"

"No, Polly," my mum's answer was firm and I knew I would get no further with my pleading. "Once your bedroom is fully sorted and tidy then you can have a wander round the town if you wish."

"I think I will ask Jamie to come with me, then," I suggested. I really wanted to find out from Jamie whether he had found out where his dad's truck had gone to last night.

"I'm afraid Jamie will be unable to go out today either." This was my dad answering, who had been sat quietly eating toast.

"Why not this time?" I exclaimed, finding that my hands were picking at my sleeve again. I didn't want to sound angry, but sometimes I just can't help it. "He said they had finished all their unpacking ages ago. That's why he came to help us last night."

"Terry told me last night that they will be out all day today. He will be going out of town, trying to sell his truck and finding a smaller car more suitable for small town life."

This sounded like a very strange reason to me, but I said nothing. I clenched my hands in frustration and sighed. I didn't mention what Jamie had said about the truck going into storage, or the fact that we had saw it drive past last night without Terry driving it. I had a feeling this was yet another thing my mum and dad were keeping secrets about. But why they wouldn't want me to see Jamie, I didn't have a clue.

"Okay, Dad," I said resignedly. I excused myself from the breakfast table in a bad mood and sulked off to my room to finish off my unpacking.

I had calmed down a lot after five minutes of pulling books out of boxes and placing them in alphabetical order on my shelves. I had even come up with a rational explanation for what my mum told me about the truck being sold. Terry must have found out there was nowhere to store a truck long term so had made the decision to sell it. It explained why the truck was seen driving around – there was nowhere to store it. It had probably parked up outside our house later last night for Terry and Jamie to drive off again this morning. They probably were driving around at this minute looking to find a new car. It was one less thing to worry about anyway. Now I just had to try and figure out where Sara and Naz were staying. The town had appeared quite small from the top of the valley the other day, so surely it wouldn't be that hard to locate?

"Looks like I'm going to go exploring on my own then," I mumbled to myself. "It can't be that hard to find a pair of twins in a small town, surely?"

As it turned out, it took me a lot longer than I was expecting to find Sara and Naz, and the day went a lot, lot stranger than I was expecting.

9

"Be back before six, Pol. I don't want to have to call a search party!"

My dad ruffled my hair playfully as he said goodbye and I took my first steps out of the house. I looked at my watch. It was twelve thirty which gave me five and a half hours to do some exploring. I glanced up at the left castle in the distance, which my mum had said belonged to an Irish family called O' Neill, and guessed I could probably walk that distance in an hour, maybe an hour and a half if the hill was steep. In the blazing hot sunlight the castle looked a lot grander than it had in the night time. I think I could even make out a huge tree in front of it, but that could have been my imagination. From where I stood on my front lawn I couldn't see the other castle – Jamie's house was in the way.

Seeing this house reminded me of something I wanted to do. I knew that my dad had said that no one was going to be in, and I had finally convinced myself he wasn't lying, but I wanted to make sure. I jogged over to the front door of Jamie's house and knocked loudly three times. There was no reply and after thirty seconds I knocked again, this time a little louder. There was still no reply, so I shrugged my shoulders and turned back towards the street. I got half a dozen steps before I paused and spun round suddenly, staring at the window of Jamie's house. I could have sworn that I saw the curtain twitch out of the corner of my eye! I stared intently at the red curtains in the ground floor window nearest to the front door. The curtains were drawn, which was unusual at this time in the afternoon, but they didn't move again.

If they even moved at all, I thought. *And it's not that unusual that the curtains are still shut. They would have probably left early in the morning when it was still dark outside.* I hated it when my mind thought rationally when all I wanted was to find something out of the ordinary going on.

"Oh well," I muttered to myself. "Exploring on my own it is then."

In the glorious summer weather, the town of Wolfwich was like a picture postcard. All the houses I passed where painted white and all the lawns were cut short and I didn't see any litter cluttering the streets. Even the cars that were parked outside some of the houses seemed shiny and new. It appeared that I lived on the main street of the town, as it was very long and straight, and it appeared to lead straight to the hills leading to both the castles and beyond.

The road was narrow and it occurred to me then that there must be a very complicated one-way system for traffic in place throughout the town. After five minutes of walking I passed a small playground with some swings and a slide. It was completely deserted. Having noticed this it suddenly dawned on me that I hadn't seen a single child at all today. In fact, the only people I had seen today, apart from my parents, were an elderly couple sat on a bench in their garden. Even the roads had been eerily clear of traffic.

"Strange," I muttered to myself. I stood still and listened. Perhaps there was a fair or something going on which had attracted the majority of the population. All was silent. Even the birds I could see were soaring silently across the sky as though the town itself was asleep and they didn't want to wake it.

Now that I had noticed this eerie silence, and complete lack of activity going on, I began to notice other little things which began to freak me out. As I continued walking, in almost every house that I passed, the curtains in all the windows were drawn. In the houses were they were open, the houses appeared to be empty. I reached a junction upon which there was a small shop on each corner – a butcher's, a book shop, a sweet shop and a hardware store – and they were all closed.

"I'm in a ghost town," I said and shivered. "Where are you, Sara and Naz?"

My idea which I had set off with – that I could ask passers-by if they knew of any new-comers to the area – now seemed daft. There was no one to speak to. The old couple I had passed had only stared at me and smiled when I had asked them.

I was approaching the end of the houses on my street now. I crossed another thin, one-way road and the hills that had seemed pretty distant just half an hour ago now loomed over me. The two castles stood menacingly high above me. If there was a thunderstorm, now would have been a perfect time for a roll of thunder and a flash of lightning.

The road I was following continued far off into the distance, between the hills and out of town, but I had walked as far as I was going to go on this road.

To my left, on the other side of the road, was a large wooden gate with the faded word *"O' Neill"* carved into the front. To my right was an iron gate with the word "Marten" wrought from the metal and painted in gold. Beyond both of the gates were twisting and steep paths that wound their way to each respective castle, perhaps half a mile or so away.

I looked at the O' Neill gate and up to the castle apprehensively. There was indeed a tree at the top of the hill, a great oak tree, but it didn't appear very inviting. Even though we were in the height of summer, the tree appeared to have no leaves on it at all. Now that I was here, having lost hope of finding the twins just by wandering the deserted streets, I began to feel nervous. Why was I even thinking of going up there alone, and also without a clear reason for doing so in my head?

Something that my mum said occurred to me then: *The two families are sworn enemies and they won't be seen in the same room together.* I imagined two people, one from the O' Neill family and one from the Marten family peeping out of their respective castles, keeping an eye on each other, and I shivered.

"I only want a closer look," I said to myself. "If the gate is locked I will turn back."

I touched the iron gate beside me and closed my eyes to build up my courage. I pushed the gate, and surprisingly it opened easily with no resistance. I was going to walk through and continue the steep trek up the path when a familiar noise made me pause and look up the road which led out of town. It was the noise of a vehicle approaching. Ordinarily this wouldn't have been enough to arouse my attention, but it had been the only vehicle I had heard all day. I gasped as the vehicle in question appeared over the horizon – it was the distinctive green truck belonging to Jamie's dad!

"They mustn't have found a car after all," I said out loud and waved at the truck as it approached. The first thing I noticed which disturbed me was that there was no one in the passenger seat – Jamie wasn't in the truck! The second thing that really disturbed me was that it wasn't Terry driving the truck, but some stranger. Terry was bald, and this guy driving the truck had wild-looking long hair. I double checked the number plate as the truck strolled past me towards town. TEZ 51 – it was definitely their truck. I forgot all about heading up towards the castle and ran after the truck, waving my hands frantically as I did so.

10

My head was pounding, the same thoughts running through my head as I chased the truck. *Where has it been? Where is Jamie? What's going on?* The truck slowed down. It wasn't because of my frantic waving, but because the truck was turning. It turned left and gave me a chance to get back to within a dozen feet before it got back to its steady speed. Either the driver was completely oblivious to my presence or he was ignoring me! I continued to wave, but the truck was getting further and further away, and I was getting slower and slower as I ran out of energy. I saw the truck take another left turn and decided that I would walk to this turn on the slim chance that it might have parked up somewhere – otherwise it looked like I would have to give up the chase.

For once today, it seemed that my luck was in. There were no roads that turned left and the only place the truck could have turned was into an open gateway, above which was a sign – *"Larry's scrapyard – We Take Your Trash For Cash!"*

The yard was vast and littered with piles and piles of metal objects, ranging from sinks and fridges to rusty cars and engines. The place didn't seem to fit in with the tidy image the segment of Wolfwich I had seen today offered. At the back of the yard, almost hidden by a mountain of metallic debris was what I was searching for – the truck had finally stopped!

I entered the scrapyard and walked nervously amidst the piles of junk. I had barely got ten metres when the man with the long, wild hair appeared from the side of the truck and began to approach me!

Okay, what should I say? I thought in a panic. *What have you done with Jamie and his dad, and why have you stole their truck?* No, that was a little too aggressive; the guy could be a raving lunatic.

I backed away and was preparing to run, when the man held up his hand and called out, "Hey kid! Hold on a sec!"

I did as he said. I don't know if it was because I was frozen in fear or because I realised I was too tired to start running again anyway. The man stopped a few feet away from me and I was amazed at how tall he was – he must have been about nine foot tall, and as wide as one of the large fridges I could see rusting away just to my right. I imagined he could probably have picked up that fridge with just one of his bulging, muscular arms. I gulped and waited for his anger. He would probably throw me out of the scrapyard just for trespassing.

"Hey there! Larry's the name, and this is my scrapyard! I don't see many kids round here, what's your name?" The man's voice was surprisingly high and jolly and he smiled with a huge cheesy grin.

"I'm Polly Peartree and I don't seem to see any kids *anywhere* to be honest."

I was surprised at my own bold reply and the huge man laughed, holding his sides as he did so. When he had stopped laughing he looked intently at me with squinting eyes.

"Peartree, eh? You wouldn't be related to the great Alfie Peartree, would you, by any chance?"

I don't think I had ever heard my dad being referred to as *"great"* before.

"My dad is Alf Peartree, yes," I admitted, feeling bemused in the way this conversation was going. This guy was supposed to be an angry, raving lunatic!

"Ho, ho. He was a legend back in the day! The things we used to get up to when we were lads!"

I remembered a name that Mum had mentioned to me in the car on the way to Wolfwich, and I said sarcastically, "Along with Viktor Marten and, er, Rav Ahmed I suppose?" Hearing the names of Sara and Naz's dad and the other friend my dad mentioned earlier took Larry into another fit of laughter.

"I knew he would have told you all the old tales. Good times, eh?"

"Er, yeah," I didn't have the heart to tell Larry that I hadn't heard any of my dad's tales. Besides, I had something more important to ask him at that moment. "Erm, Larry. Can I ask you about that truck you just brought in?"

Larry turned round and looked at the green truck. "Ah yes, I was a bit naughty there."

"Nuh ... Naughty?" I stuttered. I was dreading what he was going to say next.

"Terry popped in a few hours ago, he's another of our old school pals as you well know." He winked at me as he said this. I smiled nervously and waited for him to continue. *""Larry,"* he said to me. *"I have abandoned a green truck in the moors beyond town,"* he said. *"Big smily face on the side, you can't miss it! I want you to come and collect it after dark and dispose of it for me. After dark, mind"* he said." Larry paused and looked at the truck again, maybe to check it hadn't suddenly disappeared. "It was naughty of me, but I couldn't stand leaving an unattended vehicle alone in the moors like that. I couldn't wait until dark. I went to collect it an hour or so later and here I am now." Larry grinned at me again, his mouth wider than ever.

So, if I was to believe Larry, Terry had abandoned his truck in a place called the moors, rather than sell it in order to buy a car. Would this bizarre truck business never end? If I was to trust what Larry said, and I really did think he was telling the truth, I still had one question that needed answering. "So, where did Terry and his son Jamie go without the truck, Larry?"

Larry looked at me as though I had asked the stupidest question ever. "Why, back home of course. Where else would they go?"

I remembered the twitching curtain that I had convinced myself was just my imagination. I remembered all the other houses on my street with either curtains drawn or the houses being empty. I remembered the streets and the playground being completely deserted and no children to be seen anywhere.

Were Jamie and his dad hiding in their house along with countless other kids in their homes? Were Sara and Naz being hid away too, and why was I allowed to wander around freely if that was the case? Was I perhaps making yet more mysteries out of nothing when there were very likely some perfectly rational explanations?

My head was filling up with unanswered questions and I needed to get home quickly. My parents had answers and I was going to confront them, whether they wanted me to or not!

"I gotta go, Larry!" I exclaimed suddenly and I found that I did have the energy to run away after all.

11

I ran all the way home, fuelled on adrenaline and nerves. I considered walking up to Jamie's front door and shouting that I knew he was in there, but decided that that could wait until later. I went through my own front door instead, panting heavily from the long run. I expected both of my parents to welcome me home, but I stood in the hallway getting my breath back for over two minutes and all was eerily quiet.

Not here too, I thought gloomily.

"Mum? Dad?" I called out as I began to walk around the large house. My parents had done a good job in completing the unpacking and tidying up while I was away, but there was no sign of them anywhere.

I was now in my own room. With the bed and wardrobe and all my belongings it looked a lot more homely, but at the moment it didn't feel homely. It felt like a deserted haunted house at the funfair. I looked in the mirror built into my wardrobe, at the scared looking girl that was my own reflection. I had long messy hair that a comb could never do anything with. My face was beginning to fill with spots, I was too tall for my age and even with the jeans that I always wore, I still couldn't hide my knobbly knees. I turned aside from the mirror and looked out of the window at Jamie's house. In the upstairs window opposite mine, the blinds were down. There were curtains drawn in all the windows I could see downstairs and even the back door had a blind over the window. It really did appear as though somebody didn't want anyone looking in.

"I'll get to the bottom of this," I muttered.

I headed back downstairs, meaning to go outside and investigate next door's house. When I got to my front door I noticed the little door set into the stairs to my right, and realised that there was one room I hadn't searched yet – the cellar which Dad said he was going to convert into his new work area.

"May as well check it out," I said as I tried the small door to the cellar and found it unlocked. It was dark and cold and smelled faintly of damp in the cramped stairway. I felt around for a light switch and finally found one, but it barely changed the level of gloom. The cellar itself was vast, by far the largest room in the house. I saw several lamps scattered around the room in the dim light and I walked around and plugged them all in to give the space a little more illumination.

"That's more like it," I said and surveyed my dad's new and improved workshop. It was dominated by a large stone table that must have been here a long time before we had even moved in. On this were many different types of scientific apparatus, from microscopes and computers, to jars full of strange coloured liquids and half-built mechanical devices.

"Very nice," I muttered. I had always had a love for all things scientific. "But no one is here and so the mystery continues."

I had been walking slowly around the table and I was now at the far end, furthest from the stairs. Just as I began to head back towards the stairs, a scratching noise against the wall just to my left made me freeze. Although the lack of windows in the cellar was a little disorienting on my bearings, I was sure that this would be the wall facing Jamie's house.

Someone, or something, was scratching on the other side of the wall. It was a slow, deliberate noise. A sound very like a fingernail would make continuously dragging itself across a rough stone wall. Jamie's house must also have a cellar and someone was in there now. Perhaps they were trying to get my attention. I walked over to the wall and put my ear to it. The scratching continued and I could now hear something else as well. A little further off, as though in the same cellar I could hear a familiar, haunting sound. It was the sound of a boy crying. Two different noises, in two separate parts of the cellar next door – there was more than one person down there.

"Jamie?" I called out loudly, my head still touching the wall. "Terry?"

Both the scratching and the crying stopped at the same time. There was silence for a long moment and then I heard a familiar voice, getting louder as it approached me on the other side of the wall.

"Polly? Don't come over here Polly. I don't think you will like what you see."

"Jamie? What's going on? Can you hear me okay?"

There was a pause and then, "I hear you Polly."

Jamie's voice was really close now, his head, like mine, had to be touching the cellar wall on the other side.

"What's going on, Jamie?" I could hear sniffing, as though Jamie was still crying. "Who was scratching down there? Is your dad okay?"

Another long pause, as though Jamie was thinking hard about something. "I don't know where Daddy has gone, but he has left me down here."

There was a distant thudding noise and then I heard Jamie again, still really close. "Ooops," he said and then he started giggling childishly.

What's going on over there? I thought as another thud and then a tinkling noise of breaking glass interrupted the giggling. "What is down there with you Jamie? Is it a dog?"

"Not a dog, Polly!" Before I could say anything else, Jamie spoke again. "If you promise not to be frightened you can come and see, Pol!"

"I promise, Jamie," I said, though my heart was already thumping triple the normal speed in my chest. "Won't the door be locked?"

Jamie giggled again at something unseen. "There goes the other one!" He exclaimed suddenly and I heard another scraping noise, a little like a sack being dragged along a dusty floor. "The door isn't locked Pol. Daddy said you might pop in to see me when I'm ready for you, and I think I'm ready now!"

I felt very confused right then. First I could hear crying and scratching, and then I could hear laughing and thudding, and now Jamie admitted that he was not even locked in and was expecting me.

"I'm coming, Jamie," I said, feeling both dread and curiosity as to what could possibly await me in next door's cellar.

12

The front door was indeed open, but I felt apprehensive about entering the house without anyone there to let me in.

"Hello?" I called out as I sneaked into Jamie's house and shut the door behind me. The house seemed to have the same layout as my own but was a lot less cluttered. I tried the cellar door and found it unlocked as Jamie said it would be. "I'm coming down, Jamie," I shouted down. "Is everything alright?" I added nervously.

When Jamie replied, he spoke slowly. His voice sounded different somehow from just a few minutes ago, slightly deeper perhaps. "I'm okay, Polly. I might not look okay, but please promise not to scream."

What's going on here? I thought once again.

"I ... I'll try, Jamie."

The stairs down to Jamie's cellar were a lot brighter than my own, so bright in fact that I had to squint a little so it wouldn't hurt my eyes. I reached the bottom of the stairs and paused. Jamie was just round the corner. I could hear him humming to himself and I could also hear something else – the sound of something being dragged slowly across the floor...

Okay. Here goes. I took a deep breath and turned into the cellar.

I didn't scream, but I did put my hand to my mouth, and I think a little squeal might have escaped from my lips. Jamie was sat on the stone floor at the far wall where we had spoken just minutes before. The first thing I noticed about him was that his face was a deep green and his hair, only yesterday a beautiful blond, was now grey and wiry. The second thing I noticed, and I was amazed this wasn't the first thing I noticed, was that his arms were missing. He was wearing a white T-shirt and the sleeves hung loosely against his chest. Well, I said his arms were missing but that was a slight lie. I could see his arms perfectly well. They were crawling across the floor a few feet away from Jamie with a life of their own, heading towards me in fact. The green hands were each moving like a spider, dragging the green arms that were attached behind them like a sack of treasure. The arms ended in a stump, but thankfully there wasn't any blood, or I really would have screamed.

"Oh my," was all I could manage to say.

"Hi Polly. Don't mind me, I'm completely *armless,*" said Jamie and burst out laughing.

I couldn't help but smile at this poor joke. One of the arms had almost reached my feet. I skipped nervously away from it and jogged over to Jamie. There was a lampstand lying on the floor with a smashed bulb between me and Jamie, so I jumped over this too.

"Er, what's going on?" I asked. Jamie's arms had turned around now and were heading towards me once again. I tried to ignore them and the dragging noise that they made and stared at Jamie instead.

"Dad says I'm a zombie," stated Jamie matter-of-factly. "I think the green skin and detachable body parts was probably a giveaway," he said and giggled again.

What do you say when your neighbour has just told you he is a zombie? This wasn't a conversation I was expecting to have today.

"Er, I thought you had to be dead to be a zombie?" Was all I could suggest.

Jamie's arms had found each other now and had stopped just in-between me and Jamie. To my surprise, one of the hands grasped the other detached arm and placed two fingers on its wrist – it was checking for a pulse!

"Nope, I'm still alive," said Jamie. I laughed at this and Jamie joined in. "Dad says that this is a special town and that kid's come here every ten years and they change into something special."

"Into zombies?" I gasped.

"No, not all zombies. All sort of different things. Dad says that there is a family of trolls up the road."

"Trolls? Really? Do they hide under bridges and stop goats passing and stuff?"

Jamie giggled at this, "I don't know. I think they turn into stone, or something."

"I wouldn't like that!" I exclaimed. This was getting too surreal and I began to wonder if I had perhaps fell asleep when I had returned to my room and this was all a bizarre dream. "I wonder if I'm going to change into anything. I don't feel any different at the mo."

Jamie stared at me with interest as though trying to spot any unusual changes I might have missed. "Dad said that all the kids here will become something special, so I think you should just wait and see."

"A town where everyone can be themselves." I said, remembering the unusual slogan I saw on the welcome sign when I first arrived.

"Yeah, Dad said that too!" Exclaimed Jamie. One of Jamie's arms was now on his lap. To my surprise, it jumped up, wriggled up Jamie's sleeve and attached itself again with a loud pop! Jamie revolved this re-attached arm a few times and grabbed his other loose arm which was lying near his feet. He shoved it up his other empty sleeve and sighed in relief as it slotted back into place.

"Ah! That's a relief. I haven't quite learned to control my body parts yet, they pop out when they choose." Jamie was now brushing off his dusty fingers on his T-shirt, leaving a dark smudge. "I cried a little when my arm first fell off, but I'm getting used to it now I think."

I'm not sure that I could have got used to something that strange happening to me so quickly, and I told Jamie that. I was still convinced this was some very strange dream.

"Dad said that it would be normal to feel like that too, but he says you soon get used to it."

"Where is your dad, by the way? Did he tell you where the truck went last night? Why is he leaving you here all alone right now?" I had so many questions that I didn't know where to start. I knew that according to Larry, his dad had been getting rid of his truck for some unknown reason, but I wondered where he was now. Could he be somewhere with my parents too?

"Well, I think I will answer those in reverse!"

Jamie said. "Dad says I have to confront this on my own because I have to get used to it and he didn't want me to run crying to him every five minutes. He told me I was a zombie very shortly after I got home last night so he gave me lots of time to prepare!"

I wondered how you would prepare yourself to be a zombie, but I didn't say anything.

"That sort of answers the second question too," Jamie said and giggled again. "The whole truck business quickly fell out of my mind when I found out all this zombie stuff."

I think in that situation it would have completely gone from my mind too.

"And as for where Dad is right now, he told me this morning that there was some trouble with the werewolves," Jamie said simply.

I stared at Jamie in disbelief. Given that I was staring at a bright green zombie at this very moment, it shouldn't really have surprised me that there could be werewolves in the town too, but it did.

"Werewolves?" I asked.

"Yeah. Dad said they had to be kept somewhere safe during the full moon, which it was last night and will be tonight too, he said," Jamie paused to stare at me.

I kept repeating the word "*werewolves*" under my breath.

"I guess the truck mystery was solved last night actually, now that I remember. He told me the werewolves were picked up in his truck last night and deposited to wherever they have been took."

So there were werewolves in Jamie's dad's truck

last night! The truck had drove off to pick these werewolves up while we were packing, and we had saw the truck again an hour or so later. It was a one way road, so this must have been after the werewolves had been picked up and they were headed to wherever they were headed. There was a full moon last night, but had it come out before the truck drove off that first time or after? I honestly couldn't remember, but I think it was after. So that meant that the truck had picked up some scared kids who were going to transform for the first time. Were they still human when we saw the truck drive past later that night? I think the full moon had appeared by then.

I shivered at the thought, still chanting the word "werewolves" as though it was a magic incantation. Had the wolves / children still been in the truck when Larry passed this morning, or had they been dropped off in those moors that he had mentioned? I was about to mention what I saw earlier to Jamie when a thought suddenly popped into my brain unbidden.

The missing word wasn't witch after all.

The missing word? And then it hit me. The missing word from my mum's telephone conversation. We thought it began with a W. *We joked that it could be witch, but could it actually be werewolf?*

"I think I know who the werewolves are!" I gasped, and Jamie looked at me in wonder.

"You do?"

"Sara and Naz! I can't believe it! My two best friends! Sara and Naz!"

"Seriously?" Asked Jamie. "I guess it makes sense

that it would be someone that Dad knew. Do you think they will be alright?"

Neither of the twins enjoyed being in enclosed spaces. I remembered camping in my old back garden last summer and both Sara and Naz got increasingly nervous being zipped up in the warm, cramped tent. I tried to imagine them being cooped up inside the back of a dark truck, possibly with no idea what was going on.

"I think I might know where they are being kept. Do you think we should try and see them?"

Jamie's face lit up when I said this, "Yeah, and I can see my dad too. He will be so proud that I have changed so quickly!"

"Okay Jamie, but I think we should try not to be seen at first. Just in case."

"Our first stealth mission," whispered Jamie, then we both burst out laughing. Jamie stood up and shuffled unsteadily as he moved slowly on his big, green, bare feet. I took his hand to offer him support and we headed up the cellar stairs.

If this *was* a dream, I really wanted to wake up, and fast.

13

There were a couple of things I needed to do back at home first, so I led Jamie over to my house. I checked my watch - it was quarter past five. My dad had told me to be back home before six, so my first task was to see whether either of my parents had returned home yet. A quick shout at the front door told me the house was still deserted, so that at least made it easier for me to go back out on our *"stealth mission"*. The second task was to get my rucksack. I checked it still had my voice recorder and my Amaze-All-Portable-Science experiment kit stashed inside, then I lugged it down to the kitchen where Jamie was waiting for me. I packed the rest of the space in my bag with two small bottles of fizzy pop, four packets of crisps and a packet of chocolate biscuits from the kitchen cupboard.

"Er, zombies do eat normal food, don't they?" I asked Jamie, hoping that he wouldn't reply that he had a craving for brains or guts.

"I could eat fifty cheeseburgers right now!" Exclaimed Jamie and as if to prove this, his stomach growled mightily. We both giggled at this and I took out two more packets of crisps and handed one to Jamie and ripped one open myself.

"Just one more thing then we can be off," I said through a mouthful of salt and vinegar. There was a large magnetic whiteboard on the fridge for leaving notes. It usually said interesting things such as

"Remember to get cheese," or, on school days, *"Pol, remember your PE kit!"*

Today it was unusually empty. I quickly changed that, and finding the pen lying just by the microwave, I left my parents a quick message:

> *Mum, Dad,*
> *I know that Jamie is a zombie and Sara and Naz are werewolves. I am off with Jamie to see Sara and Naz now because they will be scared all alone in that truck.*
> *Polly.*
> *PS: I don't think I am changing into anything unusual. I don't know if this is a good thing or a bad thing so I can't wait to see you so we can chat about this.*

My quick message complete, Jamie and I set out into the still deserted street to see if we could find my best friends.

With Jamie still feeling a little unsteady on his feet and me supporting him, the walk down our street took a lot longer than when I first went out earlier in the day. Although the route was yet again mainly deserted, we noticed a few signs of life that weren't there last time around. More and more curtains could be seen twitching as curious kids or maybe their parents peeped out at the girl walking along with a zombie.

"By tomorrow, the kids won't be afraid to come outside, and the streets will be full of zombies and ogres and trolls and all sorts," said Jamie. "I don't think any of the kids are locked in, they are just afraid to go outside. Afraid that they are different," Jamie continued, speaking wisely and beyond his years.

"Yeah, hopefully, and Sara and Naz will be out there playing too," I agreed.

When we reached the playground that was completely deserted just a couple of hours ago, we both stopped in our tracks. It seemed that a couple of kids had already gathered the courage to venture outside. They were both sat on the swings and they stopped swinging when we stopped. One of them was a very tall and hairy boy with a face with a twitching red nose. I don't know what sort of creature he was, but he reminded me of a giant white mouse. The other boy was a lot shorter, perhaps three feet tall. He had pointy ears and bright red hair. I guessed he might have become an elf. I waved at the boys and they waved back smiling.

"Should we see if they want to come along with us?" I asked Jamie.

Jamie shook his head. "I would love them to come along, but I think their parents are keeping an eye on them," Jamie pointed with his head to the garden of a house a little further up the road. A group of four adults were stood at their fence, drinking cups of tea and watching over the two children on the swings.

"I guess you're right," I said and we made our way down the road. We waved at the parents as we passed and they waved cheerfully back at us.

It is indeed a friendly community, I thought to

myself.

We finally reached the junction which led away from our street and towards Larry's Scrapyard fifteen minutes later. I looked at my watch again - it was half past six. Although the sun was a few hours from setting, it was sinking, and was now as low as the spires of the Marten castle on the top of the hill above us. It took another five minutes to reach the scrapyard, and to our dismay, the gate was shut and chained heavily! The metal railings that surrounded the rest of the scrapyard were high and very sharp – there was no way for us to get in!

"Hey, our truck is in there!" Exclaimed Jamie, pointing to the back end of the yellow truck which hadn't moved all day.

"Yeah, Jamie. That's where they are keeping Naz and Sara. Just because they are werewolves, it doesn't make them dangerous!" I shouted this last sentence, perhaps hoping someone in the scrapyard guarding the twins would hear me.

To my surprise, I got a reply a second later. But it wasn't from inside the scrapyard and it wasn't from Jamie. It was from behind me!

"If you are looking for werewolves, you are looking in the wrong place."

I whirled around suddenly and was face to face with another kid of around about my age. He was tall and skinny and was so pale with such bright red lips I initially thought he was pretending to be a clown. He was wearing a black waistcoat with a red shirt underneath and tight black trousers.

"Eh? Who are you, and how did you sneak up so quietly?" I asked, feeling flustered, my heart beating rapidly from the surprise.

The boy held out a pale hand with long bony fingers. "I'm Stefan. You didn't hear me because I flew here."

"Flew?" I asked and took the offered hand out of politeness.

"Yeah, I flew from that castle up there. My name is Stefan Marten and I'm a vampire."

14

"A vampire!" I exclaimed, and then, "You live up there?" I pointed up to the castle above us where the lowering sun had now reached the crest of the hill.

"Yep. All of my life, ever since I was twelve."

"Ever since you were twelve?" I asked sarcastically. He barely looked twelve and a half.

"How old do you think I am?" Stefan asked me and he grinned, showing some very sharp teeth.

"Er, thirteen?" I suggested, being generous.

Stefan laughed and slapped his thighs. "I'm forty two this year! Lived here for thirty years now!"

I looked at him in disbelief. Stefan noticed my sceptical look and added, "From the age of thirteen onwards, we vampires age slowly. Very slowly in fact. I might look more like a teenager in a hundred years!"

"Normally I would say I don't believe you, but today is a day for suspending belief, I have discovered."

Stefan laughed again at this. "Yeah this happens every ten years or so in Wolfwich. The older generation call it *The Day of Change.*" Stefan emphasised these last words dramatically with wide hand gestures as though it had become a dance. "Hey!" He cried out suddenly. "What is your zombie pal doing with his arm?"

I turned back to the gate to see Jamie throwing one of his disconnected arms through a gap in the metal gate. "What are you doing, Jamie?" I asked, walking over to the gate.

"Just gonna get my arm to find the key to this gate!" Jamie whispered. His arm must have got stronger or gained some intelligence in the few hours since it last was detached – it was no longer dragging itself along in the dirt, but *"walking"* upright on Jamie's fingers!

"I've already said that if you want to get in there looking for werewolves, then you won't find anything," Stefan said as he too approached the gate.

"My friends are in that truck," I said and pointed to the distant vehicle.

"They *were* in the truck. They are *now* in the Shack."

"The Shack?" I enquired.

"A sturdy wooden hut. Boarded up and secluded and used to hold werewolves for centuries now."

Another phrase from my mum's recorded phone conversation came to me then: *"Let's hope the boards are strong enough this time..."*

Any doubts that I had that the twins were not actually werewolves and I had jumped to the wrong conclusion were now gone instantly. "So, you know where this hut is?" I asked Stefan.

"Sure, I'll take you there if you like," Stefan smiled and I smiled back at him gratefully.

"So, Dad is at the Shack too?" Asked Jamie, who was watching his arm get gradually further and further away as it walked on its own through the scrapyard.

"Yeah, I guess so," Stefan answered. "It is generally guarded by a few people when werewolves are sent up there."

"My parents must be up there too, and Sara and Naz's parents. It's gonna be hard seeing the twins without being seen." I said, thinking out loud.

"It won't be hard to get quite close though," Stefan pondered. "They will be guarding the hut to make sure no one gets *out*, they won't be thinking anyone would want to get *in*."

"That's true, we'll think about that when we get closer, eh?"

Stefan nodded. Jamie was still watching his arm with his head touching the gate.

"Can you get your arm back, Jamie?" I asked.

"If you can't I can fly over and grab it for you?" Offered Stefan.

Jamie looked at us both and giggled again. "I want to see you fly Stefan, but I think I can get my arms to come back to me now. I was just watching to see how far it would go."

Jamie whistled loudly and his arm, which had got perhaps thirty feet and was gradually picking up speed, stopped suddenly and turned on its fingers. "Here!" Ordered Jamie, as though talking to a pet dog. To my surprise and Jamie and Stefan's delight, the fingers marched themselves back at double the speed and jumped through the gate back towards their owner.

"Okay then, Stefan. Lead the way to the Shack!" Declared Jamie with authority with both arms pointing down the road and we all laughed.

Stefan explained that the Shack was deep in the

moors beyond the town. This made sense to me as this is where Larry was asked to collect the truck.

"But why would the truck need to be sent to the scrapyard to be disposed of?" I asked, curious. I was glad that most of the mysteries surrounding the truck were finally solved, but this one still puzzled me.

"You probably don't know much about werewolves, but when they are going through the change into a wolf for the first time the smell is absolutely awful," explained Stefan as we walked slowly back towards the junction which led down to the moors. "Imagine the smell of wet dog multiplied by a thousand." Stefan paused, then added, "With two werewolves together and them being nervous, make that multiplied by five thousand. That smell will never wash out of the truck so it's better to scrap it."

"Eurgh," I said, trying to imagine the smell.

"Wet dog smell," said Jamie and laughed.

"So, what is it like living in a castle, Stefan?" I asked as we finally reached the junction and turned right, heading towards the moors beyond town.

Stefan sighed and looked up at his home. "It's lonely to be honest. I have the place to myself most of the time, apart from Rhubarb and Loretta, and neither of them speak much."

"Rhubarb and Loretta? Are they vampires?"

"No. Rhubarb is my pet lobster and Loretta turned up yesterday. She's a poltergeist."

"A Poltergeist?" I exclaimed.

"Well, a poltergeist in training, to be honest. She is getting some practise in, smashing a few plates, drawing on the chalkboard, that sort of thing."

I couldn't help laughing at this - it sounded so absurd, but Stefan was looking deadly serious. This made me laugh even more, and because it didn't take much to make him laugh, Jamie joined in too. "Sorry, Stefan, I've never heard of a poltergeist in training before."

"The ghouls and ghosts and poltergeists always seem to find their way to my castle to get a bit of practise in. They have kept me entertained over the years!"

"Are your parents not around?" I asked, and then I remembered a name Dad mentioned in the car the other day and added, "Was Viktor Marten your dad?"

Stefan looked at me as though he was surprised that I knew the name. "My parents went away travelling a few years ago and I haven't heard from them for a while."

Stefan was studying my face carefully. "Yes, I see why you asked about Viktor, you look just like your dad, Miss Peartree."

I gasped, for one second amazed how he could know what my dad looked like, before remembering that Stefan was a lot older than he looked. "Viktor wasn't your dad, of course! You both must have looked pretty much the same age back then. Was he maybe your brother?"

"Nicely thought out, er, I don't think I know your first name yet?"

"Oh, yeah, it's Polly. Or Pol if you like. Polly Patricia Peartree," I realised I was rambling a little and blushed.

"Great name, Pol!" Said Stefan. "Yeah, Viktor is my twin brother. We were both best friends with your dad. What adventures we had back then!"

So my dad was also best friends with twins back in his school days! And it seemed he was also friends with Jamie's dad and Sara and Naz's dad back then too. It really was a small world we lived in, with everything seeming to be connected.

I really needed to chat to my dad one day about all these *"adventures"* he seemed to be having as a kid. Although, having said that, I was currently walking with a vampire and a zombie heading off to visit some werewolves, so hopefully I was getting into a few adventures of my own!

"So, where is Viktor now?" I asked, shaking myself out of my thoughts. "Did he go off with your parents too?"

We had just passed the gates that led up to the two castles, and before Stefan could answer, a high-pitched screaming noise suddenly broke out in the air in front of us.

"Eeeeeeeeeh!" It began, getting higher and higher in pitch, and then a shadow popped into existence a few feet away from us.

"Oh, no, it's Betty!" Stefan exclaimed. He stepped in front of myself and Jamie so that he stood between us and the shadow.

"Betty?" I asked. I held Jamie, who had his hands in his ears to keep out the high pitched wailing.

"Betty O' Neill is a banshee," shouted Stefan over

the noise. "Lives in the other castle up there."

Before I could reply to this, the wailing suddenly stopped and the shadow suddenly transformed into a short girl dressed all in black. She wore a black short skirt, black boots, black lipstick, she had jet black hair, and covering her body and arms was a black cape. So here was one of the mysterious inhabitants of the O' Neill castle facing one of the Marten family! I held my breath, half expecting a fight to break out.

"Yes! It's Betty!" Her voice wasn't quite as high pitched as the wailing, but it was pretty close. "You're off to the Shack? Well, I've been to the Shack! I made it the Screaming Shack for a while! Eeeeeh! Eeeeeh!" I think Betty was laughing but I really couldn't tell. She began to sing a song then, spinning around with her cape and jumping on the spot in a bizarre dance.

"Two girls are in the hut,
But will the door stay shut?
Full moon in two hours or one,
And by then the wolves will be gone!"

Betty began her very annoying laugh again then. Jamie had put his arms back down, but his detached hands had remained in his ears – very convenient earplugs! Jamie probably would have said they were very *"handy"* if he could hear me at that moment.

"What have you done, Betty?" Stefan asked calmly, advancing slowly to where Betty was, still spinning around and jogging on the spot as though she couldn't keep still.

"Had a little chat. And maybe loosened a few boards! Eeeeeh!"

Stefan suddenly lunged at Betty to try and grab hold of her, but she was a fraction of a second too quick. With a popping noise she turned into a shadow again! The shadow moved at lightning speed towards me and Jamie, and before anybody had time to react, Betty had reappeared behind us and she pulled Jamie's hands out of his ears!

"Mine!" She shrieked before turning into a shadow once again. Her high voice trailed away as we saw the shadow move up the hill towards Marten Castle. "Now for a little fun with Lorettaaaaaaa!" She shrieked before the noise faded away.

Before anyone else could react, Stefan jumped into the air, but he didn't land again from the jump – he had already turned into a bat and was heading towards his castle after Betty the Banshee.

15

"My hands!" Wailed Jamie suddenly, beginning to cry. He raised his arms to his eyes but the green stumps where his hands should have been weren't very useful, so I searched in my rucksack for a tissue and wiped his eyes for him.

"We need to get my hands, Polly!"

"Yes and we need to be quick. I think Betty has done something at the Shack, and we might need to warn whoever is down there! Oh, ham and jam, that Betty is a nuisance!"

"She is, Pol. We are gonna have to go up to the castle now. We will never find the Shack without Stefan and I'm not very handy without my hands!"

I knew he would make use of that joke at some point and I agreed with him. It was a little later than I had planned it, but I was finally going to see Marten Castle up close.

It was a steep climb and very tiring. What probably took both Betty and Stefan a few seconds, took myself and Jamie half an hour. It might have taken ten minutes less had Jamie not lost his foot half way up the hill, and we had to run after it as it rolled and bounced back down again. The vast front door was open when we finally reached the top, but I knocked timidly on the ancient oak anyway before stepping over the threshold into the castle.

"Hello? Stefan?" My voice echoed around a cavernous hallway, brightly lit by what must have been a thousand candles. My shadow danced and flickered along the stone walls to the left and right of me. Ahead was a grand stairway leading up to a vast archway and beyond this a corridor leading off to the depths of the castle. The hallway was strangely quiet. I was hoping to hear Stefan shouting or even Betty's annoying wail, but all was deathly silent.

"Come on, Jamie, let's find Stefan and your hands!" I declared jovially, trying to sound braver than I actually was feeling.

"Right behind you!" Was Jamie's enthusiastic reply. If he was nervous he didn't show it either. We ascended the stairs side by side and then made our way slowly down the corridor. There were closed doors at regular intervals on both sides of us, but we continued going straight on, not wanting to get hopelessly lost. There was a bright light at the end of the long corridor, but it didn't appear to be getting any closer as we trudged slowly on and on.

I felt a slight breeze behind me and I turned around.

"Did you feel that breeze, Jamie?"

"It has gone colder, I think," was Jamie's reply.

It was indeed colder and the breeze had gotten stronger – my messy hair was now brushing against my face. There was a small vase on a pedestal to our left and it now began to wobble precariously. Suddenly the breeze got stronger still and the vase flew from the pedestal. It didn't fall to the floor as I was expecting but rose higher into the air as though grasped by something invisible. The vase stopped in mid-air and then it began to rock gently back and forth. It was as though the invisible presence was taking aim with the vase and preparing to launch it hard. And this is exactly what happened to the vase. It flew at speed across the corridor, heading for the opposite wall. I flinched, anticipating the vase to smash against the wall violently, but the smash never came. Instead there was a popping noise and a familiar screeching noise right in my ears.

"Eeeeeeeeeh! Not this time! Eeeeh! Eeeeh!" Betty had appeared suddenly and caught the vase before it could be destroyed!

Now another familiar noise was approaching at speed - a flapping sound of fast moving wings. A bat had arrived, and before I could blink, Stefan was now standing in the increasingly crowded corridor!

"Too late again Stefan! Eeeeh!" Betty shrieked. The breeze had now gone again, and Betty disappeared once more to chase after it, her shadow zooming along the walls at a dizzying speed. Stefan looked at the shadow and then back to me and Jamie.

"It's hectic here! Betty is being more of a nuisance than usual, as you can see!"

Apart from the annoying screaming, all I saw Betty do was stop a vase from being smashed. It seemed a strangely nice thing to do. "Err, what's going on?" I asked, perplexed.

"The breeze you felt then, that was Loretta the poltergeist. She wanted to smash the vase but Betty stopped her," explained Stefan gently.

I still looked a bit confused. "It saves you sweeping up doesn't it?" I asked.

"It's not good for Loretta's self-esteem. Poltergeists like to smash things up or scare people by moving the furniture around. With Betty stopping all Loretta's attempts at being a good poltergeist, then Loretta is going to get upset." Stefan looked at me to see if I now understood him, which I think I did. "And an upset poltergeist is a dangerous poltergeist," he added.

"Dangerous?" Asked Jamie.

"They will try to smash bigger and bigger things. A television. A fridge. I've heard tales of a very angry poltergeist lifting an entire house with everyone in it once!"

We both gasped at that. I didn't fancy finding myself in a flying castle with an angry poltergeist and a screaming banshee.

"What can we do, Stefan?" I asked.

"Well, if we can't catch Betty, we are going to have to banish her!"

Before I could ask Stefan what this meant, Betty's screech returned, coming from down the corridor beyond the bright light in the distance.

"Come on!" Urged Stefan, and he ran down the corridor. I followed him as fast as I could and Jamie wasn't too far behind me. When we had got to the brightly lit room at the end of the corridor, we were already too late. Loretta and Betty had already rushed off to another area of the castle to continue their personal battle of wits.

The room we found ourselves in appeared to be a

living room. There were three massive sofas in one half of the room, surrounding a huge flat screen television on the wall. In the other half of the room was a large round table and on the table was a fish tank. The water was very murky in the tank, so I couldn't see any fishes in it. There were two other things on the table and Jamie spotted them straight away.

"My hands!" At the sound of his voice, Jamie's hands sprang into life and jumped off the table in unison. They sprang onto Jamie and were very quickly re-attached. "Aaaah!" Sighed Jamie in relief and flexed his fingers and massaged both his wrists.

"I guess Betty got bored of those now she has Loretta as her entertainment," said Stefan.

"So," I said and clapped my hands, "How do we go about banishing Betty then?"

Stefan sighed. "Well, that's the question isn't it?" He declared. "Firstly we will have to get her out of the castle and keep her out for a good five minutes. That will be the hard part as doors and windows are no barriers for a shadow."

That would indeed be a challenge. "If we manage that, then what happens?" I asked.

"Well, then we perform a banishment charm. It is a simple yet powerful chant which requires four voices to complete."

"Four?" I thought for a few seconds. "So Loretta can speak can she?"

"Not exactly, but she does have a special talent which can come in handy for this occasion."

"Go on," I urged, intrigued.

There was a bang and a clattering noise above us. It appeared that Loretta had finally got one small victory over Betty and smashed something.

"Good girl, Loretta!" Stefan shouted to the ceiling. "Well, Pol. Poltergeists also have a special little known talent. They have the ability to manipulate living creatures that might not normally have the ability to communicate with human beings. In other words, they can give them the brief ability to talk!"

"That's cool," I announced, impressed. "So who do you have in mind?"

Stefan was walking over to the fish tank. "Why, Rhubarb of course!"

Rhubarb? And then I remembered — Stefan's pet lobster! "A lobster?" I asked, incredulous.

Stefan reached into the murky tank and pulled out a fat, bright red creature with little beady eyes. It seemed to be grinning at me, but that was probably my imagination.

"Cool!" Exclaimed Jamie, and then he looked puzzled. "My dad says that lobsters are not normally red until they are boiled."

Stefan laughed at this and nodded. "This is a special lobster, Jamie. It comes from a magical lake near my home town a very long way away. There are mermaids and mer-kings and queens in that lake too!"

"Whoa!" Jamie and I were both impressed by this.

Rhubarb was placed on the table where he began to scuttle around in a circle, snapping his huge claws. It made a sort of *"glub"* sound, as though it was already getting in some talking practise.

"So, firstly, we need to get Betty out of the castle," I announced, bringing us back to the task in hand.

"Yep," said Stefan. "Any ideas?"

"I'm *stumped*," declared Jamie who had pulled both of his legs from his blue shorts and was sat on the floor. Stefan laughed but I looked at Jamie sternly and he quickly attached his legs again.

"Sorry, Pol," Jamie looked sad momentarily then brightened up again suddenly. "Could we just give her some of our snacks and ask her to leave politely?"

Stefan shook his head. "She will probably eat your snacks then continue to torment Loretta. She will leave eventually when she is bored, but it won't be fair on Loretta."

"I might have an idea. Thanks Jamie!" I shouted suddenly.

Jamie mentioning snacks reminded me that I was carrying my rucksack. I took it off and pulled out my Amaze-All-Portable-Science experiment kit and rummaged inside it. Yes, a plan was forming in my head now.

"Betty is basically human isn't she? She does eat and sleep and everything else eventually?" I asked Stefan as I searched for what I was looking for.

"Yeah. Of course, she is partly human in that respect."

"Okay. Loretta will just have to smash them all. Betty can't stop water once it starts flowing. How to get her to swallow it, hmm." I realised I was mumbling to myself and both Stefan and Jamie and even Rhubarb were staring at me.

"Okay guys," I whispered, just in case Betty had decided to spy on us. "Here is my idea."

16

Inside my Amaze-All-Portable-Science experiment kit were several potions and powders which I had created myself. These had various uses, varying from making fruit drinks fizzy to itching powder for people you particularly didn't like. There was one specific potion I had in mind, one which worked very quickly indeed and would get Betty desperate to get out of the castle if Loretta did her part of the plan correctly.

Stefan grinned and Jamie began to giggle as they heard what I was planning.

"So, you want to give Betty a laxative potion and get Loretta to flood the toilets here so she has no choice but to rush off home. I have to say, it's simple but genius!" Exclaimed Stefan.

"*Give Betty the runs! Give Betty the runs!*" Jamie chanted and began clapping his hands.

"It's quite a good idea, but with one major flaw," I conceded. "I don't know how we are going to get Betty to swallow the potion. I doubt we could simply offer her a drink."

"Hmm," thought Stefan. "She might drink it if we left it out somewhere but it's a bit of a risk and we might be waiting for hours." Stefan shook his head sadly.

Jamie suddenly stood up from one of the sofas he was lounging on and reached into the pocket of his shorts. "Will this be any good?" He asked. He had pulled out a small yellow water gun and was aiming it carefully at my face.

"It might just work!" I exclaimed. "You would have to be very precise with it, and you will only have one chance to fire the potion down Betty's throat, Jamie."

"I can do it!" Said Jamie excitedly. "What's the plan, Pol?"

Now that we had a method of giving Betty the potion, the rest of the plan was straight-forward. I explained it quickly and hoped that it would all work as I hoped.

The nearest bathroom in the castle was located on the floor above the living room and Stefan led the way, jogging quickly, full of enthusiasm. We all stopped just outside the bathroom to catch our breath and survey our surroundings. I had asked for somewhere where there were plenty of items for Loretta to attempt to smash, and somewhere for Jamie to hide with his gun and this was a perfect location. There were several pictures on the wall of the corridor we stood in and just opposite one of these – a portrait which could have been Stefan or his twin brother – was a large plant in a huge pot, the perfect place to hide.

"Okay, Jamie. Get comfortable and remember there is only enough potion for one shot. So make it count!"

Jamie saluted theatrically and got into position behind the plant pot. He aimed his water gun, now fully loaded with what he had decided to call *"Poop Potion"*, at the portrait and waited.

"Ok Stefan," I said, "Get Loretta."

Stefan nodded and took a deep breath. He shouted Loretta's name as loud as he could, so loud the pictures on the wall actually shook a little. Within seconds we felt a familiar breeze, followed swiftly by a less enjoyable but equally familiar screeching noise.

"Loretta, smash my picture!" Stefan exclaimed and pointed. The picture rose instantly into the air, almost to the ceiling and fell at speed back towards the ground. As we were hoping, the picture didn't make it to its destination and was caught by Betty just inches from the thick green carpet.

"Eeeeh Eeeeeh!" Laughed Betty. "Try har — gleuuurgh!"

Betty never finished her sentence as Jamie expertly fired the potion into her wailing mouth. The spray continued for a good five seconds — she was bound to swallow enough of it for the potion to have an effect within two minutes!

"Okay, Loretta!" Called out Stefan. "Flood the toilets! Every single one! Do the *en suite* ones upstairs first then come back here. Betty won't be able to stop you!"

"We'll see about that!" Shouted a soaked Betty as she vanished and went after Loretta's breeze.

"Okay, Loretta won't be long," I declared. "Good job Jamie! Did you hear her gurgling down the potion you fired right down her throat?" I imitated Betty, quite effectively I thought, and Jamie and Stefan laughed.

"Yeah, that was funny!" Exclaimed Jamie. Above us was a crash and a scream and this was followed thirty seconds later by another crash and a louder screech. Loretta had done her task upstairs and was going to be with us for our toilet at any second.

"Brace yourselves for the wailing once again!" Said Stefan with his fingers in his ears. The breeze that was Loretta stormed past us and burst open the bathroom door. Betty was already in the bathroom, stood in front of the last remaining toilet, dripping wet from the flooding that must be occurring upstairs.

"No you -" began Betty, but the force that was Loretta was too strong and the banshee was swept aside. The toilet didn't just break, it exploded. Water gushed everywhere, flooding the tiled bathroom floor and gushing out onto the corridor. I ran further along the passageway with Jamie and Stefan to keep out of the way of the puddle that was forming on the carpet.

Betty was really angry now. Her screaming was worse than ever as she jumped up and down angrily, splashing in the puddle in her black boots. Just when I thought I couldn't take the incessant screaming any longer, Betty stopped suddenly and held her hands to her stomach. We could all hear the grumbling noise that suddenly erupted from her belly, and Betty's face went suddenly very white.

"She's gonna explode!" Giggled Jamie under his breath.

"What have you done!" Screamed the banshee. She looked to the destroyed toilet and down at her tummy and realisation dawned on her. She groaned and held her stomach tighter. She looked at Jamie, who was giggling and waving his water gun around in the air and she screamed once more. In an instant, Betty swooped over to Jamie and grabbed the water gun off him and then suddenly disappeared once again with a pop! Her shadow trailed down the corridor where there was an open window and Betty vanished outside.

"My gun!" Wailed Jamie in shock.

"At least she's gone, Jamie," I said soothingly to the zombie. "We have to keep her out now!"

"Okay, now let's get back downstairs," said Stefan, already heading down the corridor. "We need to do the banishment charm quickly before she gets back! Come along too, Loretta, we need your help!"

The breeze seemed to push us along as we hurried back downstairs to the living room. Stefan walked over to the fish tank and pulled out Rhubarb, who had been returned there when we had rushed off upstairs earlier. He placed the large lobster down on the floor and told us all to gather around in a circle, which we obeyed, Stefan on one side of Rhubarb and Jamie on the other with me opposite the lobster.

"Okay Loretta, if you don't want to see any more of Betty then we need your help once more!" The breeze flew around us swiftly, ruffling our hair, which we assumed meant that Loretta assented to help us.

"We need Rhubarb to talk," said Stefan gently. "I know this will be tiring for you but it won't be for longer than five minutes, then you can relax."

The breeze flew around us once more and then stopped. I kept my eyes on Rhubarb and something amazing happened. First, the lobster began to swell and then it began to glow, an unusual neon green colour.

There was an unusual humming noise and then the glow faded and Rhubarb returned to his original size and colour.

"Nothing happ-" I began, but then Rhubarb stood up suddenly on his back legs (I'm not sure if they are legs or arms, but they were short and stubby and very strong either way) and his beady eyes fixed on me. It was a very human look and was very disconcerting coming from a lobster.

"My tank needs more shells for decoration, Stefan," said the lobster. It sounded as though his throat was full of water as he spoke, but he certainly spoke good, clear English. "Just thought I would say that to you while I still can!"

Stefan laughed at this and Jamie joined in, finding a talking lobster hilarious.

"So is this Loretta speaking or Rhubarb?" I asked, a little confused.

"I'm Rhubarb," answered the lobster plainly.

"Loretta doesn't have a voice of her own but she can persuade creatures that they have a voice for a limited time," explained Stefan. "We need to start the banishment charm now, so can we all hold hands and, er, claws in a circle please?"

Since Rhubarb only came up to our knees even when stood up, we sat down so Stefan and Jamie could hold his claws comfortably. I tried not to giggle at the sight and concentrated instead on what Stefan was saying.

"To whoever may be listening," began Stefan in a loud commanding voice, "Hear my charm to banish one

Betty O' Neill from this, the Marten Castle."

Stefan looked around at the circle to make sure we were all holding on to each other. "Okay," he whispered, "Repeat after me loudly everything I say and don't let go of the person next to you."

Stefan began the charm slowly, and we repeated what he said after each sentence.

"Hear our charm and let it be seen.
There is someone here not to be.
The power of four will make you hear.
Banish the one we loath and fear.
Banish the banshee and keep her out.
Not even to get up the water spout.
Hear our charm and do as we bid.
It is Betty O' Neill we want to be rid!"

We finished the charm and sat in silence for half a minute, not daring to loosen our grip on each other until Stefan said so. Although it is hard to describe in words, as we sat there, a feeling of calm suddenly washed over me then, and I knew the charm had worked. Stefan let go of my hand and sighed deeply.

"I've been meaning to banish Betty for ages now. Thankfully that's over with!"

"That was cool!" Said Jamie.

Rhubarb walked into the centre of our circle on unsteady feet with his heavy claws outstretched for balance. "Well guys, before I go back in the tank for a good soak, I'd just like to say thanks for letting me be part of all the fun!"

"No prob, Rhubarb," Stefan said enthusiastically. "I'll let you out for a chat again when Loretta has had a good rest."

"See ya, Rhubarb," I said and shook his claw. Jamie did the same with his other claw. We raised Rhubarb to his tank and let him jump into it himself. The lobster sank to the bottom and ten seconds later, some bubbles rose to the surface and a familiar breeze rushed around us before disappearing from the room.

"Thanks Loretta!" We all called out.

Loretta had had a busy day and was now all tired out. I was getting tired myself and could have done with a good nap, but the evening was young and there was still much to do.

17

It was eight o'clock and the sun was close to setting. Stefan had agreed to escort us down to the moors and find the *"Shack"* where Naz and Sara were being kept. We had had a quick break for some crisps, and Stefan had made us some sandwiches after Loretta had gone for her rest, and we were now walking down the steep hill from his castle.

"I hope all that damage Loretta did to your toilets won't be hard to fix," I said as we approached the gate near the main road.

"Oh, don't worry about that, Pol," said Stefan cheerfully. He lowered his voice and whispered, "It's another little known fact about poltergeists, but they like to repair the damage they do and they make great cleaners too!"

I laughed at this and told Stefan that every home should have a poltergeist. He agreed and said Loretta could come and visit anytime I wanted. I tried to imagine what my mum would say if I brought home an invisible friend, but I couldn't visualise her possible reaction.

Thinking of my mum, I wondered again whether my parents were indeed at the Shack, and whether or not it would be better to approach them and talk to them rather than trying to sneak into the hut without being seen. I had so much to speak to my parents about and I really wanted to know everything they knew about what was going on, and also whether they knew anything about me.

What I wanted to know the most was whether I was going to change into anything like Jamie and the twins and so many other unseen kids in the town. I still wasn't feeling any different, and I was still the skinny girl in jeans and checked blue shirt that I was this morning.

Stefan brought me out of my ponderings by saying, "We are at the northern outskirts of Wolfwich now. The moors start just over the crest of this hill."

He pointed ahead of us, where the road did indeed disappear over the crest of a hill less than fifty feet away. I hadn't realised we had walked so far, but far from feeling tired, I jogged up the hill to get my first glimpse of the moors. Jamie was already there taking in the view and Stefan arrived at my side a second after me. The road we were following wound its way along the hill to our right but the moors were directly in front of us. I was expecting the moors to be dull and lifeless, perhaps with lots of grey and mud and rocks, but what we were faced with was field upon field of purple flowers, for as far as I could see. Even in the diminishing sunlight I could see bees busily scurrying from flower to flower and I even caught a glimpse of a rabbit dashing across a bare patch of grass.

"It's beautiful!" I gasped, breathing in deeply the sweet scent that the flowers seemed to radiate.

"It's always a spectacular place to look at, especially at sunrise and sunset," agreed Stefan.

This reminded me of something I was meaning to ask Stefan, which had been nagging me for a while now.

"You know, Stefan, I always thought vampires couldn't go out in sunlight."

Stefan smiled at this. "I burn easily and use a lot of sunscreen, but the whole night time thing is for the older generation really. My parents are more traditional, but the rest of our family come from a more modern breed. We don't even sleep in coffins anymore! Well, not often!" Stefan laughed at this and Jamie joined in.

"What about garlic? Is it true about vampire's hating garlic?" I asked.

"Well, I can't stand it myself, it stinks!" Stefan replied. Jamie was now rolling around on the floor theatrically.

"And I suppose a stake through the heart would kill you?" I asked playfully.

"I think a stake through the heart would kill anyone, Pol," stated Stefan seriously then grinned again. "Anyway, back to business! The sun has nearly set and we have a good ten minutes to walk yet!" Stefan waded through the knee high sea of purple swiftly and I went after him, followed shortly by Jamie.

"I can't see any huts," said Jamie as he tried to keep up the pace. "It's purple everywhere!"

"You can't tell from here, but the field descends into a small valley a short way ahead and that's where the Shack is."

Stefan looked to his left where the sun was spreading out its last fingers of light across the field – it was about to set below the horizon. The full moon could be seen clearly in the sky, a pale disc just waiting for the sun to set completely to have the night all to itself.

"Quickly!" He urged, and we ran along after him. I ran into Stefan a minute later as he had stopped suddenly.

"Listen," he whispered.

I stood still and listened attentively. At first I could only hear the wind rustling though the flowers and Jamie's breathing as he rested from the run, but then it came to me – a sound both haunting and lonely, and at the same time inviting, as though it was calling me. It was the sound of howling. It was joined a moment later by another howl, the two merging to one desolate cry into the night.

Stefan didn't have to tell me, for I knew what it was instantly. Sara and Naz had transformed finally into werewolves, and from the clarity and volume of the howling, getting louder each second, they had broken free from their captivity. They were roaming free in the moors and heading straight towards us.

18

"We got here too late to warn anyone!" I whispered, dismayed with myself. The howling had stopped and everything was eerily silent, which to me was scarier than the howling.

"Let's head to the Shack anyway. We have come this far," Stefan said.

I looked around nervously. "What about the wolves? I mean, Sara and Naz?"

Jamie pointed suddenly to our right. "Look!"

Heading towards the edge of the moors, and the road and hills beyond, two black, bushy tails were pushing their way through the purple flowers like sails on the sea. They were moving fast and we wouldn't have been able to catch them, even if we had tried.

"Sara!" I shouted, but neither of the tails stopped, even for a fraction of a second. They were soon out of sight, and I wondered how long it would be before they would return or possibly transform back into the best friends that I knew and loved. I followed Stefan reluctantly in the opposite direction that the werewolves had headed.

We hadn't been walking for long when a familiar grey, bushy head of hair, followed by some red spectacles emerged over the crest of a hill directly in front of us.

"Dad!" I exclaimed and ran up to meet him. He looked both relieved and happy to see me, and he caught me as I dived into his arms.

"Polly! I was hoping you would have got here earlier, you just missed the twins!"

I was expecting Dad to quiz me on what I was doing here at this time of evening, or something along those lines so I was a little confused by his response.

"Er, you have been expecting me to come here?"

My dad laughed and his glasses wriggled on his nose. "Me and Mum know you Pol. We knew your inquisitiveness. We just thought you would have got here a lot quicker. It has been hours since we arranged for you to see that truck."

I looked at my dad with my confused look again. It was a confused look that was being used a lot recently. It seemed that for the past few days both of my parents had spoken to me in nothing but riddles and mysteries.

"Er, you arranged for me to see the truck?" I asked, feeling more confused than ever. "When Larry was driving it?" I added for clarification.

"Yeah, and I see Larry led you to Jamie, and you two bumped into Stefan," Dad said and waved at my two new friends. "I thought you would have led them here quicker though," Dad said, directing this sentence at Stefan.

Stefan looked at his feet, embarrassed. "Sorry, Alf. The plan was delayed."

Plan? My dad had planned all along on me meeting Jamie and finding my way to the Shack, and Stefan knew about it all from the start? I wasn't angry but I could feel myself getting worked up.

"I suppose you sent out Betty to torment us too as part of your plan, eh, Dad?" I asked sarcastically. It was my dad's turn to look confused and shocked now.

"Betty? No, I didn't want you to see her Pol, she's a pest."

My dad looked genuinely concerned and I felt sorry then that I had accused him of sending Betty to annoy us.

"So that was what delayed you, eh?" Dad asked.

"Betty stole Jamie's hands and then she was winding up Loretta the poltergeist so we had to banish her and it was Betty who did something at the Shack to let the twins out!" I blurted out in one quick gasp.

"Ah! I would have loved to have seen all that!" My dad chuckled. "She did help the twins get out a little bit early, although we were planning on letting them out anyway. She got there just a tad ahead of us somehow, but she didn't cause as much mischief as she would have hoped!"

"I thought you were guarding them heavily?" I asked.

"Well, keeping an eye on them, yes. You never know how a wolf will react the first few times. They spent most of the day sleeping, to be honest. They have been brilliant though, Pol. They love it!"

"Sara and Naz *like* being werewolves?" I asked, still incredulous.

"Yeah, they really take after their parents!"

"Eh?" I asked, but my dad had now moved his attention to Jamie, asking him how we had managed to banish Betty.

"Pol gave Betty the runs!" Exclaimed Jamie and started to laugh once again. My dad joined in, and this time his glasses wobbled so much that they fell off.

"I bet she is still on that toilet now, eh Jamie?" My dad asked and now Jamie was on the floor, once again in stitches. Dad waited patiently until Jamie had calmed down again and then he said, "Your dad is down at the Shack too, Jamie. I bet you have lots to tell him?"

Jamie jumped up excitedly. "Yes!" He shouted. "I'm gonna show him my arm trick!"

"I'd love to see that too, Jamie. Should we go, everyone?" Dad asked, and we all agreed to make our way to the Shack.

"Is Mum there too, Dad?" I asked. I could see the Shack now at the bottom of the hill Dad had appeared over. It was an old wooden building, a little larger than a garden shed, which was what I had been expecting, and more like the size of a decent sized kitchen.

"She is just out at the moment, but she won't be long, and then you can ask us *anything* you want to know, and this time we will tell you the whole truth."

I looked at my dad to see if he really meant this, and he looked back sincerely. "There may be a few surprises when Mum returns, but all will be revealed."

19

When we arrived at the Shack, two people I recognised were sat together deep in conversation. One of them was Larry, the giant scrapyard owner, and the other was Terry, Jamie's dad. Although I recognised Terry instantly, he had changed considerably since I saw him last. He was a large muscular man before, but now he must have been twice his previous size in terms of muscle. His skin was now dark green, darker than Jamie's was, and his bald head was full of red scabs and scars.

"Dad! You're a zombie too!" Jamie exclaimed as he entered the Shack.

Terry turned and stood up and ran over to hug his son. "Aye, that I am, kid! Must be something in the water!" Terry laughed at this and looked lovingly at his son. "You have turned out a fine looking zombie, Jamie!" He said proudly.

"Me and Stefan and Polly have been having lots of fun!" Jamie declared and proceeded to tell his dad about meeting me in the cellar.

I left them to catch up on events and looked around the Shack. Piled up in the far corner of the hut was a bundle of blankets and a large black bulky rucksack. The rest of the room was bare apart from a large gaslight on the floor which gave the dim hut just about enough light to see by, and a light blue bathrobe and a baseball cap hung at the back of the door we had just come through, which Stefan had shut behind us. The bathrobe looked strangely like one of my mum's, and the baseball cap looked just like one I lost a few years ago, both of which struck me as very odd in this empty, wooden, windowless room. I couldn't see any sign of a loose board anywhere; perhaps it had been secured back in place.

My dad had took a seat on the floor to the right of the door and I moved over to join him. Stefan joined Jamie and listened to him talk animatedly to his father, going through the day's adventures in minute detail. Terry was listening with delight evident on his face at each word in Jamie's retelling of how we banished Betty. Larry was walking up and down the room idly. I had forgotten how tall he was; his head was almost to the ceiling!

"Why is Jamie's dad a zombie now, too?" I whispered to my dad.

"He has been a zombie ever since he was Jamie's age. Coming back to Wolfwich means all our old identities come back eventually," Dad explained. My dad didn't look any different than I remembered him, just like myself, so did that mean I took after him in some way?

"What about Mum?" I asked. "Has she changed?"

"You'll see," Dad said and then chuckled to himself as though he had said something that amused him. "Well, you will find out soon," he finished and chuckled again.

"And Sara and Naz's parents? They aren't …"

I didn't need to ask the question because my dad's smile answered it for me. What had he said just before we entered the Shack? *That the twins really took after their parents?*

"Yes, they are werewolves too. Just stretching their legs as we speak, no doubt!"

All this new information was becoming a bit overwhelming for me, and yet, I still didn't know much about myself. "And what about me, Daddy?" I asked.

Dad looked at me sternly from above his glasses, a look he liked to give when he didn't want me asking more questions. "I'm not going to answer any questions till your mum gets here, Pol, so just wait awhile."

I looked at Dad sulkily for a second and then headed silently to where Stefan was sat at the far side of the room, close to Larry.

"It's been quite a day, eh, Pol?" Stefan asked.

I sighed, tiredly. "It has, Stefan. But I don't think it will be over till Sara and Naz are found. Don't you think we should go looking for them?"

Stefan shook his head. "I believe that's what your mum is doing right now. They will be back soon."

I stared at Stefan in disbelief. "My mum is chasing after a couple of werewolves? I don't think I have seen her run in my life!"

Stefan had a strange sort of smile on his face, as though he knew something I didn't know. It seemed that everyone apart from Jamie was keeping secrets from me, and it was infuriating. "You know more than you're telling, don't you?" I asked. "You helped my dad to get me here without telling me, and you know something secret about my mum too," I said accusingly, but not meanly. I paused, a crazy idea popping into my head at that moment. "Mum isn't a werewolf too is she?" I whispered.

Stefan smiled at that but shook his head. "No Pol, but she knows a lot about werewolves and has some useful skills in finding runaway ones like the twins."

"Tell me more!" I urged Stefan. He was shaking his head and smiling. "Please," I continued. "I can't stand all these secrets!"

"Sorry, Polly. You will find out everything very soon, I promise."

I was going to continue pestering Stefan to try and coax some information out of him, when at that very moment an ear-shattering howl silenced everyone in the room. This was followed a split second later by another howl.

"Very, very soon indeed. Here they come now," Stefan mused.

We all looked at the door in apprehension. There was a sound just outside of approaching footsteps and then a scratching and banging at the door as something or a couple of somethings jumped and pawed at the wood, keen to get in. A familiar voice called out gently, *"Down, girls,"* and then the door opened. Two huge, great hairy dogs, pitch black in colour with fiery red eyes, stepped into the room, panting heavily and straining at the leads that were holding them firmly back.

"Down girls!" The familiar voice that belonged to my mother repeated the phrase again more firmly. I could hear my mum clearly. The voice resonated around the room loudly, but I couldn't see her! The two leads that held the werewolves were pulled taut and seemed to float in mid-air – no one was holding them!

"Mum?" I called out, confused. The door closed again and my dad picked up the bathrobe and cap from behind it.

"Here you are, honey," he said, holding out the robe to no one I could see and taking hold of the leads. The robe moved from Dad's hands and swirled around on its own and suddenly filled out, taking on a female form. The cap floated upwards and stopped a little bit above the top of the bath robe where the shape of some slim shoulders could be made out. What I had just witnessed suddenly clicked into place then and I gasped. My mum was wearing the bathrobe, and she was invisible!

20

"Mum!" I exclaimed.

I ran over to the invisible figure in the bathrobe and awkwardly embraced her. It was an unusual feeling. I could see right through where my mum's face should have been, yet I could smell her perfume and feel her hands on my back!

"Hey, Polly, nice to see you," my mum laughed and then suddenly her little nose appeared, floating on its own between the bathrobe and the cap. Her red lips popped into view next, followed by the rest of Mum's face and body. She wasn't wearing anything else other than the bathrobe, and I gasped.

"You went outside completely naked, Mum?" I asked.

"I wouldn't be completely invisible otherwise! You forget you're naked when you go invisible to be honest!" Seeing my mum invisible, or not seeing her, gave me yet more questions I wanted answering. I asked the one that now bubbled up to the top of my thoughts.

"Will I be able to turn invisible too?"

"Well, Polly, if you haven't noticed yourself going invisible yet, then I'm afraid you won't become an invisible girl like me. At your age you wouldn't be able to control it and you would be fluttering in and out of visibility at any moment. It was embarrassing when I was your age I can tell you!"

My parents both laughed at this, sharing yet more memories of a strange childhood I had been unaware of all of my life.

"So your invisibility came back today, just like Jamie's dad has become a zombie again?" I asked, trying to get all these strange facts in order in my head.

"Yeah, pretty much," Mum replied. "I could do it every now and then back in our old home, but only if I concentrated really, really hard. Here it is as natural as breathing or itching your nose!"

"Bet it can come in handy being invisible!" I exclaimed dreamily. There were so many things that I would do if I had that talent, and I felt a little disappointed that it seemed unlikely that I was to become an invisible girl like Mum.

"It can be very useful indeed, especially for keeping an eye on people," Mum said.

I looked at her in disbelief. *Was she suggesting what I think she was suggesting?*

"Mum? Have you been following me?" I asked.

Mum stared at me, perhaps trying to judge whether I was angry with her or not. I wasn't angry, but it felt a little disturbing to find out you are being secretly watched. "Just from a distance, Polly. Dad was against it, he said you could handle yourself, but I just wanted to be sure. I didn't interfere, even when Betty made an unexpected appearance!"

"You could have helped with our banishment charm at least!" I said finally. "We had to get a lobster to help us!"

My mum looked genuinely confused at this.

"Banishment charm?" She asked. "That must be what all that banging was in the castle! I kept my distance and I didn't follow you inside, though I was tempted a few times! You *have* had a busy day!"

"I have Mummy, but will you promise not to sneak around following me again?" I asked, adding politely, "It was thoughtful of you, but I'm fine, especially with Stefan and Jamie around."

My mum nodded at this. "Okay Pol, you are right. With Stefan and Jamie around you are in safe hands. Anyway, I believe you may have something you want to ask me?"

For a second I didn't know what she meant, but then I glanced at my dad who was sat patiently waiting for us to join him, and I asked my mum what I wanted to know.

"Do you know why I don't seem to be changing, like the twins and Jamie and the other kids?"

Mum motioned me towards where Dad was sitting cross legged in the corner of the room to the right of the door. "Come on then, Polly, let's sit down and have the chat you have been dying to have all day."

I sat opposite my parents who sat next to each other so I could see them both as we spoke. Sara and Naz, who had been padding around the Shack aimlessly, approached me and sniffed me for a few seconds then walked away again. I couldn't tell the difference between the two dogs, they both looked completely alike. I had always recognised Sara because of a birthmark on her nose, but there was no such mark that I noticed on these werewolves. It occurred to me that perhaps these two wolves could in fact be the twins' parents, so I asked my mum this.

"No Polly, when Anita and Rav return, you will see the difference!"

I looked around the room at my two other new friends. Jamie the zombie and Stefan the vampire were chatting to Jamie's dad happily, laughing and joking. I returned my attention to my parents and asked the question once again that I most wanted to know the answer to.

"So, what am I going to become, Daddy?"

Dad pushed his glasses back up on his nose – they were once again dangerously close to falling off. "Well Pol, I think I'll begin by asking you a question, if that's okay?"

"Okay," I assented, curiously.

"We know you have met Jamie, a zombie, and Stefan, a vampire, and even Betty the banshee, and a poltergeist. Have you saw anyone else who has changed to something special?"

I thought back and remembered the playground with the two boys playing. "I saw a tall lad, with lots of white hair and a red twitchy nose. And I think I saw an elf. And Jamie said there is a family of trolls down the road. And Larry. Is he a giant or just very tall? Oh, and Mum the invisible woman!" I smiled at my mum, who smiled back warmly.

"Larry is indeed a giant, although quite a short giant really!" Dad said and chuckled. "The white haired boy would be Dave's son. He's a yeti," Dad added thoughtfully. "Anyway, Pol. All these creatures -

vampires, zombies, yetis, giants and trolls. They are all popular in stories, are they not?"

I agreed with my dad, wondering where he was headed with this question.

He continued, talking slowly. "Well, you may not have believed it before we moved, but you certainly do now, but all these stories are based around fact. You have seen that zombies and poltergeists and werewolves are real and not just cool story characters."

Dad paused and reached into his pocket and pulled something out that I couldn't quite see. I saw a glint of metal and then it disappeared as he closed his fist over it. "There are some story characters that keep turning up in different forms that are not supernatural and are ordinary human beings. But they are just as important. They have special talents which they use to affect the story, sometimes for bad uses but mainly for good uses."

Dad paused again and looked at Mum. She nodded for him to continue. I was looking as confused as ever. *Was Dad trying to tell me that I was just an ordinary human in an extraordinary town?*

He continued once more. "One such character is sometimes described as bumbling and clumsy, sometimes as mad or crazy, but they are always important. The character I'm talking about is the scientist." Dad paused here then added with a grin, "We have been descended from a long line of mad scientists, it would seem."

My dad stopped talking to see how I reacted. *So was my dad saying I was just an ordinary girl that liked science?* I knew that already. I wasn't sure if I should feel disappointed or relieved.

"So, I'm a scientist?" I asked, finally.

"Not just any scientist, Polly. While you live here you will find you can achieve things normal scientists would only ever dream of," Mum said encouragingly.

"What do you mean?" I asked, intrigued.

"Show her, Alfie," Mum said to my dad.

Dad opened the hand that was concealing the metal object to reveal what looked like a small silver badge in the shape of a leaf. There was a tiny red circular button in the centre of it. "I created this just a week after I came to Wolfwich at your age."

"What is it?" I asked. My heart was speeding up excitedly, I really wanted to press that button.

"Take my hand Pol and we will find out."

Just as I was reaching over for my dad's hand, there was a sudden thud at the door which made me jump. This was followed by a loud bark. Naz and Sara reacted excitedly to this, bounding over to the door with tails wagging. They began yapping and whining like puppies.

"That will be Anita and Rav!" Mum said as Larry paced over to the door with his long legs and let the two wolves in. There was a definite difference between the two wolves that entered the Shack and the two younger ones waiting at the door – the twins' parents were huge – they must have been at least as tall as my shoulder and they barely fitted through the door, squeezing into the Shack one at a time! One of them was slightly smaller than the other and had white fur – I guessed correctly that this was Anita. Rav had the same black fur as his daughters and he whined happily as the twins pounced on him and they all began to roll around playfully.

This had been barely going on for longer than thirty seconds when all four wolves suddenly stopped rolling around and they stood completely still. They all began to whine in unison. The wolves suddenly began to shake uncontrollably. Their fur began falling to the ground and the whining got louder.

"The moon is going," my mum whispered. "They are changing back."

21

"The blankets!" Mum shouted, and Terry, who was nearest, dived towards the bundle in the far corner and picked up three thick, black blankets. He threw two over the twins and one massive blanket over the larger shivering wolves. He did it just in time – the bulky shapes under the blankets began to change. Long bare arms popped out at either side of the blankets and long bare legs grew out from the bottom. Within thirty seconds two girls with long blankets over their heads, like pretend ghosts, were stood in each other's arms in front of us. Their parents were huddled together under one blanket, looking embarrassed in front of all of us watching. The twins pulled their heads out of their blanket while remaining covered and I finally got to see Sara and Naz in human form in this mysterious little town of Wolfwich. Their long black hair was a mess, bits of twigs and leaves were sticking out of it like a pair of pincushions. Both of the twins had very red eyes. They looked extremely tired.

"How are you, girls?" That was the twins' dad, just a head visible from above the large blanket he shared with his wife.

"Dad!" The twins exclaimed together.

"You never said you were werewolves too!" Naz cried out.

"We could smell you out there, but we couldn't find you!" Sara said and twitched her nose as though the smell was still in her nostrils. The birthmark had returned so I could tell them apart once again.

"We're glad that you got back safe. We didn't think you would get out of the Shack today," Anita said with concern.

"Sorry Mum!" The twins said together and yawned. They looked exhausted.

"Let's get you dressed and we can get some sleep," Rav said. "Terry, pass the rucksack please?"

Terry passed over the large black rucksack that was with the blankets and Rav fished out four large onesies that he shared out between them. The family all got dressed under their blankets and when they emerged I had to laugh – their onesies all had a picture of a wolf on them!

"Polly!" The twins shouted in unison, as though noticing me for the first time.

I went over and hugged them both. They still had a smell of dog to them but I didn't care one bit. I was just so glad to see them.

"We have so much to talk about!" Naz said.

Sara scratched her head vigorously. "I think I have fleas," she stated simply.

"I still have the urge to scratch myself with my legs," added Naz, and I laughed at that.

Sara and Naz both yawned again, a long and loud whine. It was an infectious noise and I soon found myself yawning too.

"You know, I think we should all get some sleep, it has been a long day for us all," I said and the twins agreed wholeheartedly.

We hugged again and then Sara and Naz sat down with their parents. Their mother handed the twins a pillow each from their rucksack and the twins were both fast asleep in under a minute of placing their head on their pillow. My parents hadn't brought me a pillow or a onesie, but it didn't matter. Tiredness had swept over me and I was asleep shortly after the twins, led peacefully against my mother.

I awoke to the sound of snoring all around the hut. Although the Shack was windowless, a thin sliver of light coming from a gap beneath the door suggested to me that the sun was up. A glance at my watch told me it was seven in the morning. I sat up carefully so I wouldn't wake my mum, who was snoring gently, and looked around. Everyone who was here last night was still here. Jamie and Stefan were dozing back to back, Larry was slumped in a corner; his snores were the loudest in the room, the twins were still fast asleep, as were their parents. Terry was asleep quietly in the other corner where the blankets used to be. Dad was the only one in the room other than me who was awake. He waved at me and I waved back and smiled.

"Morning," I whispered.

"Morning, Pol," Dad replied. "How is my little scientist?"

I remembered our conversation last night about the truth about myself. I didn't feel any cleverer this morning at any rate, but I didn't tell my dad that.

"Okay, I guess. I thought most of yesterday was one long dream, but this is still the Shack and not my bedroom, so this must all be real?"

"It sure is. Jamie is still a zombie, and the twins are still werewolves!"

"It's so hard to believe," I said, wiping sleep from my eyes. "Will they be changing like that every full moon then?"

"Every night while they live here," my dad replied.

"Every night?" I asked. "There's not a full moon every night. It goes in cycles doesn't it?"

"There's a full moon here every night. It's a magical town if you haven't already guessed. Did you not wonder why there was a full moon on the welcome sign on the day you arrived?"

I thought back to the car journey here, and of the welcome sign we had passed. "I thought it was the sun in the picture."

Dad chuckled at this and shook his head. "Nope, a full moon every night here, Pol."

"It's a strange place. I hope I can get used to it," I said as I looked around at the sleeping forms around me.

"But wonderful too I hope, eh, Miss Scientist?"

I grinned at this name and then suddenly remembered something from last night. "We never got round to pressing that button!" I exclaimed.

"Well let's try it now while no one is looking!" Dad said and took out the leaf-shaped badge from his pocket. "Take my hand, Polly."

I took my dad's hand apprehensively and closed my eyes.

My eyes had been barely shut for three seconds when my dad said, "You can open your eyes now. I have pressed the button."

At first I thought that nothing amazing had happened. We were still sat in the wooden hut, my dad staring at me and grinning. But then I noticed that the room had gone completely silent – the background sound of the snoring had gone, even Larry's heavy, noisy grunting snore had been silenced. I looked around and everyone was still there but they weren't moving – it was as though they had all been frozen all at once. In fact, it was just myself and Dad who were moving in any way, even Mum was frozen with her mouth open in mid-snore.

"You have frozen everyone!" I gasped.

"I have in fact stopped time. I created this little device when I was your age. Just a few days after I discovered I was to be a scientist like you."

"Wow!" I said. I was impressed. I reached out and touched my mum's forehead tentatively. It still felt warm and soft and like a normal forehead, but my mum didn't react in any way.

"Everyone will remain frozen in time till I press the button again," Dad stated as though he was giving me a science lesson.

"Will I be able to make one of those?" I asked excitedly.

"You will be able to make anything you can imagine within time. Your creativity and knowledge is going to grow at a remarkable rate over the coming days so who knows what you could do?"

The thought of being able to stop time thrilled me and I wondered when I was going to get some of this creativity and knowledge. I tried to imagine what I would do with the ability to stop time and countless possibilities flooded my mind. I would never be late for school again, that was for sure.

Something occurred to me as I was thinking then. One of the mysteries about my parents was explained. "You and mum used this to get the packing done when I was out, didn't you?"

There was a gleam in my dad's eye as his grin widened. "We did, yes. Our secret is out now!" We both laughed at this for a while. I was convinced the noise of my laughter would somehow break the time-freezing in some way and wake everyone up, but it didn't. My dad held out the leaf shaped badge. "Want to bring everyone back to the present?"

I took the badge cautiously. *If I dropped it now and it broke, would my friends and mum be frozen in this hut forever?* I pressed the little red button and the sudden noise explosion, as everyone's snoring started up again as though they hadn't stopped at all, hit me like I had been pushed. I fell from a sitting position to a lying one and then started giggling helplessly.

My mum shifted in her sleep, but no one else stirred or noticed my little fit of giggles. I was about to hand back the badge to my dad when I was struck suddenly with an idea.

Naz and Sara were still sleeping soundly behind me, led side by side and smiling as they dreamt happy dreams. I stood up and moved towards them quickly. My dad must have realised what I was going to do because he began to get up too.

"Polly, don't -" he began, but he didn't get to finish his sentence. I knelt down in front of the twins and grabbed a handful of both of their onesies. Hoping that it would work, I pressed the red button once more.

22

My dad was frozen halfway between sitting and standing, staring at me with unseeing eyes. The room was completely silent again. Well, almost silent. The twins were still breathing quietly, so my idea had worked.

Should I wake them up or wait around for them to wake up on their own?

I decided that a bit of sunlight might do the trick and maybe a bit of noise too. I stomped over to the door clumsily, making my feet slap the floorboards noisily. I pushed open the wooden door to bring in a torrent of sunshine directly onto the twins' faces. This did the trick more than my noisy feet did – first Naz stirred, followed shortly by Sara who groaned and shielded her eyes.

"Nnnnnh," Sara moaned with her eyes still shut.

"Bright," mumbled Naz.

"Wake up, lazy!" I addressed both of the twins cheerfully. The twins both sat up, both still squinting from the intense sunshine.

"Hey, Pol! What's with waking us up so early?" Naz continued to mumble.

"I dreamt that I was a wolf running through a giant purple field," Sara said and rubbed her head.

"That wasn't a dream, Sara," Naz declared.

"Yeah I know, it feels like a dream though. What a mad couple of days!"

"I woke you up so you could tell me about it. I couldn't wait for your side of the story any longer!" I exclaimed excitedly.

Before either of the twins replied, Sara suddenly screamed and jumped backwards. She had just noticed my dad frozen in a position that would normally be impossible to stay in for longer than a second or two. "Pol, w ... what is your dad doing? He isn't even blinking!"

"Oh, I just stopped time so we could talk in private!" I declared smugly.

"You what!" The twins exerted together. They looked around and finally noticed that everyone in the room weren't just asleep but completely frozen too.

"I'll tell you my story after you have told yours, starting with your first arrival at Wolfwich," I said eagerly.

"Oh no," Naz said, shaking her head, "You can't just tell us that you just happened to stop time magically and expect us to tell our side of the story first. We want to know how you have done it first."

Sara was nodding and agreeing with her sister. She poked her mum nervously to see if she would react, and smiled when she didn't even flinch.

I could see the twins' point of view. I decided to tell them all that happened to me from the moment that I left them at the Park on Sunday evening, which almost seemed a different lifetime ago.

"Let's go out into the field first," Naz said, pointing outside. "The flowers look lovely."

I agreed with this, and, as ever, I took my

backpack with me. Sara and Naz went out in just their onesies but the weather outside was bright and warm. The field in the early morning did indeed look spectacular. It felt as though we were walking through a purple sea as we walked through the flowers to the top of the hill. We settled down here, with the Shack below us and I told them all that had happened to me.

I began with the strange circumstance of my parents having already finished the packing in record time, to seeing Jamie and his dad in the morning before setting off. I told of the trip to Wolfwich, and the unusual welcome sign on the evening of arrival, and finding out about the two mysterious castles. I told about how I was told then that they (the twins) were also to be living in Wolfwich and how I found out that Jamie was also going to be living there. Sara and Naz nodded at certain points and agreed at others but kept respectfully quiet throughout my retelling.

I told them of the incident with the truck driving off mysteriously and then driving past again that night, and then I moved on to the long and mysterious events of yesterday. I told them of the deserted town, and following the truck, and then discovering that Jamie was a zombie, and then moved onto meeting Stefan and the first confrontation with Betty. Both twins gasped at the mention of that name – they had evidently encountered her themselves. They laughed when I told them about Betty's banishment, and they were very interested when I told them the final part of my tale, about how I found out about my own true identity as a *"mad scientist"* as my dad described it. I pulled out the silver badge and told them of this morning's events with my dad stopping time and I finished my tale by saying, "So that's my mad tale. How about yours?"

The twins looked at each other and laughed. "It's not quite as exciting as your tale!" Naz said finally.

"Where shall we start?" Pondered Sara. "How about being put to sleep in the car?"

Naz considered this and nodded. "Yeah, we will start from around there," she said and the twins began recounting what had happened to them.

23

"Our parents didn't keep everything a secret to be discovered like your parents did, Polly." Naz began quietly but quickly got into her stride as her tale went on. "When we were on the motorway on that first day they told us then and there that Wolfwich was a magical town with some unusual inhabitants, and because they didn't want us to know where exactly the place was, that we would have to be sent to sleep until we arrived."

"Mum had drugged our juice bottles!" Butted in Sara.

I remembered back to my own car journey and remembered that my mum had offered me some pop and I fell asleep shortly after that. It seems I had been put to sleep too, although I wasn't told beforehand! I didn't say anything but my eyes widened in amazement.

"It must have been a strong dose because when we woke up we were no longer in the car," continued Naz. "We found ourselves cooped up in a massive steel container with our parents. It was empty apart from a bundle of blankets in one corner. There was a skylight in the roof that let in a bit of the fading sunlight."

"It was the truck!" Exclaimed Sara.

"Yeah, straight from a car to a truck," said Naz. "You know, we haven't even seen our new house yet!"

"We haven't even seen the town yet!" Sara added.

"I think you must have been asleep outside your

house while your parents waited for the truck to arrive," I suggested thoughtfully. "You set off very early in the morning according to Jamie, before his dad had collected all your belongings anyway. The truck didn't drive away from our house till early evening."

Sara and Naz thought about this, then both nodded together as though sharing the same thoughts.

"Yeah, putting our stories together it seems to make sense," Naz spoke for both of them. "I have a feeling our dad must have drove the truck from yours to ours though."

"Yeah, that makes sense," I agreed, and Naz continued with her story.

"Dad told us almost as soon as we were awake that we were werewolves and that we would be transforming at sunset."

"Quite a shock, I can tell you!" Sara exclaimed, stating the obvious.

"Yeah, I think we didn't believe them at first, but when Mum and Dad left us in the truck alone shortly after that we got scared."

"Terrified!" Sara said. I don't remember being a wolf that first time, do you Naz?"

Naz thought about it then shook her head. "No, it seems like a blank space in my memory. One moment it was getting darker and darker outside and we were panicking, trying to find a way to get out of the truck we were locked in, and the next moment it was morning, we were naked with our clothes ripped and ruined and there were thick black dog hairs all over the floor."

"And it really smelled too!" Sara exclaimed.

> >>> >> >>>>>>>>>>>>>>

"Yeah, it really did smell. It was our smell but it was still really bad! Anyway!" Naz exclaimed loudly to change the subject from the smell. "When the truck was opened that morning we were on the road just by this purple field."

"The truck must have started moving after we had transformed," said Sara thoughtfully, "We definitely didn't notice the truck moving before that."

"I don't think we even knew it was a truck until our parents opened the doors in the morning," Naz said. "When they opened the truck we were too tired to talk and we let them lead us through the field to the Shack. It really takes it out of you, this transforming into a wolf!"

"I noticed last night," I agreed. Something was nagging me about the truck again, so I brought it up once more. "If the truck drove to the moors when you were werewolves, then who was driving the truck? Your parents must have been werewolves too at the time!"

The twins both looked at me perplexed. Just when we were getting to the bottom of one mystery it pops up again, trying to confuse us!

Sara brightened up suddenly. "It has to be Larry! You saw him yourself driving the Truck, Polly, so we know he can drive it!"

"It must have been him all along!" Naz said. This made the most sense yet, so I quickly drew the twins' attention back to their tale before the whole truck mystery distracted me once again.

"As I was saying," Naz began as she resumed her tale, "We were pretty tired most of yesterday and we must have fell asleep yet again, because when we woke up Mum and Dad had gone, and a strange girl dressed all in black was standing over us and giggling."

"Let me guess. Betty!" I cried and sat up eagerly. I really wanted to hear this part.

"Yep, that annoying shriek she does constantly!" Naz did quite an impressive impression of Betty's shriek and we all laughed.

"She wouldn't shut up. She must have talked constantly for two or three hours while no one was around. We were both too tired to try and chase her away or anything."

"And she was always dancing around the Shack too, she couldn't keep still."

"Where was everyone then?" I asked. "I was expecting the place to be heavily guarded or something."

"I think they were meant to be patrolling, either to keep us in or to keep others out, but when we escaped from the Shack, they were sat on the hillside eating sandwiches!" Sara exclaimed.

"I didn't notice that!" Naz said. "Too busy running around following my nose I guess in those first few moments of freedom."

"So Betty must have told you how to get out of the Shack then?" I asked.

"She kept going on about that!" Sara exclaimed. "Going on about a board she loosened and she kept pointing to it and screeching!"

"We must have remembered it as wolves though, because we found our way out!" Naz added.

"Yeah!" Sara exclaimed excitedly. "I certainly remember that time as a wolf more clearly. What about you, Naz?"

Naz's face lit up into a bright smile. "The smells were the best. It really opens your senses up. The flowers, the air, the wind through your fur, it was heavenly!"

"And everything looked so clear!" Sara added. "The colours all looked different but I could see everything with perfect clarity, little insects, rabbits, the birds in the sky, each individual blade of grass!"

"We could smell you too, Polly!" Naz said with a grin. "And Jamie and Stefan. You all have very distinct smells, and even as a wolf I could tell that the smell that belonged to you was you."

I remembered seeing the two black tails belonging to the twins heading away from us. I had tried shouting to them but they had appeared not to hear. I asked why they never came to me when I shouted.

"We had already been distracted by then by another more powerful smell," Naz answered. "One we knew all our lives, though we had never smelled it like this."

"It was Mum and Dad!" Sara said

"Yeah, we headed in the direction we sensed them in, oblivious to any other noise. Sorry Pol, but the animal instincts just took over there!"

"Yeah, and then your mum caught us and brought us back again, Polly!" Sara said with a grin. I laughed at this and asked how she managed that.

"Well, we could smell her too, ahead of us, but we

couldn't see her," Sara began.

"It was frustrating," Naz added. "She had a really nice honeysuckle perfume on, and I could smell cheese and onion crisps on her breath but neither of us could track her down. We then noticed the leads on the floor."

"Our big mistake!" Laughed Sara.

"Yeah, although the smell was getting stronger and stronger, we edged closer because we couldn't see the owner of the smell. It was getting in the way of the smell of our parents which was getting further and further away. Your mum must have been crouched down just next to the leads because quick as a flash they were both round our necks before we could react! And that's pretty much it really, quite dull compared with your tale."

I was about to suggest that we return to the Shack, when Sara cried out suddenly, "Tell Pol about Ted, Naz. She needs to hear about Ted, I think he might need our help!"

A look of remembrance came to Naz then. "Oh, yeah, another thing that Betty enjoyed going on about," she said, and then proceeded to tell me about Ted.

24

"Before going on about the loose boards in the Shack, Betty kept telling us about some kid called Ted, who was locked in her cellar."

"Locked in the cellar?" I gasped.

"Yeah, what was that song she kept repeating? Can you remember, Sara?"

Sara started humming a tune, looking thoughtful as she murmured a few phrases to herself. "She repeated it so often, I think I might get it in a mo," she said as she repeated the same tune again and again. "Okay, I think I have it."

Sara then sung a short song with two verses in quite a sweet voice. I imagined that Betty's version wouldn't have sounded so nice, and this is what Sara sang:

"Ted is in the cellar, locked up tight,
Nowhere to hide, day and night,
Ted the bogeyman, not allowed to leave,
Uncle Rory has got the key.

Rory has the key, locked in a locket,
A chain around his neck, not in his pocket,
Ted the bogeyman wants to be free,
We're not gonna let him, hee hee hee."

Sara finished the recital and Naz applauded.

"Yeah that was it! Betty always finished it with that annoying laugh of hers though."

"Do you think it is true?" Sara asked, thoughtfully.

I thought about my encounters with Betty. She had sung a little song to me, Jamie and Stefan yesterday and told us she had loosened a few boards at the Shack, so I believed the song. I told the twins this and asked them what we should do.

"We can't let someone stay locked in a cellar, I say we organise a rescue mission!" Sara exclaimed dramatically.

"Another top secret operation!" Joined in Naz.

"I think it is going to be pretty impossible," I added, spoiling the enthusiasm a little bit. "Getting into Betty's castle, getting the key to the cellar off her Uncle Rory, whoever he is, then rescuing Ted without being seen."

Sara looked glumly at me, but Naz was grinning widely. "It will be ridiculously easy, you have forgotten something important!" Enthused Naz. I looked at her quizzically, urging her to go on.

"We are still frozen in time! We could walk right up to the castle and right up to Rory, and he won't even notice a thing!"

The simplicity of this astounded me. I had completely forgotten about stopping time! Apart from the complete absence of wind in the air and the stillness of the flowers, there were no clues that the world around us was currently frozen.

"Yeah! We could go right now, rescue him within a couple of hours and carry him back here and unfreeze time again!" I said, the enthusiasm for the simple plan returning again. The twins were already running through the fields towards the hills upon which the two castles could still be seen. "Wait up!" I called out, struggling to keep up.

We had got as far as the road leading back to Wolfwich when something went majorly wrong with our plan. The time-stopping badge, which I had placed in the top pocket of my shirt began to whistle loudly. I could feel heat coming off it and I pulled it out quickly.

"What's going on?" The twins asked together.

"I don't know," I answered. The badge had stopped whistling now and had gone cold once again.

"I think your time thingy has stopped working. Look." Sara pointed to the sky where a large bird was soaring elegantly, its wings spread majestically. It was very clearly moving; time had returned back to normal.

"That plan has gone out the window then. What now?" Moaned Naz dejectedly.

"We go back and discuss our plans with the others," I declared resolutely. "I think we will need Jamie and Stefan's help on this one."

25

We hadn't got far in our return to the Shack when my dad approached us at a run. He stopped in front of us, panting heavily.

I got my apology in quickly before he could get his breath back. "Sorry, Dad. I just wanted to chat to Sara and Naz in peace up here a bit. I didn't mean to break your time-stopper."

"It's not broke, it just has a limited time span. You can't keep time paused forever, Polly," Dad explained, still taking deep breaths; the run had really tired him out. "I didn't have time to warn you. I know what you are like. You were probably planning on doing something drastic."

I looked at my feet, embarrassed. The twins were doing the same.

"It seems you didn't get far however, so I think I'll have it back now?" Dad held his hand out and I handed the badge back shyly to him.

"Could I perhaps borrow it later? It is a handy thing to have," I asked with a smile.

"It is handy, but I'm afraid it will be out of action for a few days now, it needs to recharge. You can't mess about with time too much in one day, Pol," Dad said in a lecturing tone.

"Will we all be heading back home soon?" I asked Dad after a while as we followed him hurriedly back to the Shack.

"We will, but first we should get back before everyone wakes up!"

We headed back home just a couple of hours later. We didn't have to walk as Larry had a pickup truck which we all jumped in the back of. The truck had been hidden out of sight in the flower filled field just a few hundred yards from where the road led back into town.

On the short trip from the moors to the twins' house, I told Sara something that I had forgotten about when telling her what happened to me on the day I was travelling to Wolfwich for the first time.

"*What do you mean there is no phone signal!*" She exclaimed loudly to everyone else's amusement. She began to rant on about this for a good few minutes and I wished I had stayed quiet about it. She was quieting down a little in her rant by the time we finally arrived at the twins' house.

I had been dying to see the twins' new home, so I had asked my mum whether I could stay with them for a bit and have a look around. I also had another motive for this, and that was to make a plan for rescuing Ted. Even though I had never met him or knew anything about him at all, the thought of Ted or anyone else being locked up all day really got to me and I felt like I really had to do something about it. Especially with Betty being around all of the day, probably taunting him and shrieking. It must be unbearable and I had to do something about it!

Jamie had got permission off his dad to come along, and Stefan agreed to have a look around Sara and

Naz's new home too. They didn't know about Ted yet, but I was sure they would be willing to help when they found out.

The twins' house was in a corner of the town, set into the hill upon which Betty's castle stood. The castle in which Betty was possibly now tormenting Ted, along with her mysterious Uncle Rory. The house was large and white, similar to my own but I noticed one difference straight away – they had a massive garden. I could imagine the twins running around that garden as wolves quite happily.

The twins' parents gave us all a guided tour and it was a very impressive house. It was Sara and Naz's first time in seeing the house too and they were very impressed, although every now and then Sara would grumble something along the lines of, "Nice place, but shame about the phone signal!"

They were especially impressed with the size of their new bedroom, and it was here that I, Naz, Sara, Jamie and Stefan met after a quick lunch of fried egg sandwiches, made by the twins' dad.

"Well guys," I declared, addressing Jamie and Stefan, as we all sat on the two large beds, "It looks like Betty has been up to yet more mischief!"

Stefan and Jamie both looked at each other in confusion.

"Eh?" Asked Jamie.

"What?" Said Stefan.

I brought the two confused looking boys up to date with events, beginning with my dad's demonstration of his time-stopper. Stefan grinned broadly at the mention of this device.

"Ah, yes, I had forgot about that!" He said. "Me and Alfie had some good times with that!" I kept forgetting that Stefan was much older than he looked and he would have seen lots of my dad's inventions and been on many adventures with him. I would have to ask him about some of them one day, but for now we had our own adventure to plan!

I carried on with retelling the events of this morning and Sara recited her song again, and all she heard from Betty about Ted. I told them of our plans to rescue Ted and of our failed idea to use the time-stopper to do this.

"Not Betty again!" Groaned Jamie.

"I have encountered Rory a few times before," Stefan announced and looked around the room at us gravely. We all looked back at him eagerly. "He is not like Betty," he said. Jamie sighed at this and the twins looked relieved. "He is much worse," Stefan continued.

Jamie's smile fell and we all looked at Stefan, concerned.

"Betty might be a nuisance, but Rory is pure nasty. He is a banshee too, but without the fun that Betty has. He just doesn't like anyone. If we break into his castle, he is going to be very, very angry."

Jamie gulped and the twins looked nervous.

"Does everyone still want to plan a rescue?" Stefan asked and laughed nervously.

"I think that Betty might actually want us to help her get Ted out," I said thoughtfully.

"What?" Said the twins together.

"Eh?" Said Jamie again.

"Go on, explain," encouraged Stefan, intrigued.

"Well, like you said, Stefan. She isn't nasty, she just likes to have fun."

"She stole my hands!" Interrupted Jamie.

"Yeah, she's a nuisance, and very annoying, but I think she just wants someone to play with. She told us what she did at the Shack so we would investigate, and she told the twins what has happened to Ted. I feel she might not like what her Uncle Rory is doing at the castle either." I finished my little speech, feeling embarrassed.

"I agree, Pol," Stefan said finally. "But I don't think she will offer to help straight away. We will still have to put up with some of her annoying tricks if we get into the castle."

"So, Operation Ted Rescue," Naz declared, looking determined. "Any ideas?"

There was silence for a while as the ideas failed to materialise.

"I can use my head?" Jamie suggested eventually.

"We are all trying to use our head to get a plan together, Jamie," I said patiently.

"I mean, I can *use my head*!" Emphasised Jamie and suddenly pulled off his own head with a *"pop"* sound. He placed his head on the ground where it began to roll around on its own! Stefan thought this was hilarious, and after their initial shock, so did the twins.

"Throw me through a window and I could look around the castle for you!" Jamie announced. He looked at us from the floor, his head currently upside-down, his mop of grey hair being used as a cushion. He looked so funny like this that I couldn't help laughing either.

I decided to be brave and bring up the phone signal issue once again. "At least our parents can't contact each other by phone to keep an eye on us," I said.

Sara glared at me but conceded that I had a point. "So, we could each say we are having a sleepover at the other's house and it's likely we would get away with it?" She asked.

"Just what I was thinking! So it at least gets us out of the house without too much fuss," I replied.

"I think I can get us into the castle," Stefan stated when we had finished going through the plan of arranging sleepovers as cover for our secret mission. "The difficult thing is going to be getting the locket from Rory."

We all agreed that this was going to be the difficult part and we again fell into a thoughtful silence.

"We will have to do it at night, when Rory is asleep," Sara announced after a while.

"That's risky," I said. "He might sleep during the day for all we know."

"And what if we turn into werewolves again tonight?" Naz asked. "Anyone know if it's gonna be a full moon?"

I nodded at this, remembering what my Dad had told me yesterday. "I'm surprised your parents never told you, since it will affect you two the most. There's a full moon here every night!"

From their first reaction to this, I wasn't sure if the

twins thought this news was good or bad. Sara twitched her nose and Naz squinted her eyes at me, but they said nothing.

"When it happens, you can be our guard dogs!" Jamie suggested.

"Whatever happens, we still need a plan," I stated, feeling completely devoid of ideas.

"If only we could guarantee Rory will be asleep when we find him," Stefan pondered. "Any sleeping potion in that bag of yours, Pol?"

I thought about it and shook my head. "I'm afraid not. Besides, Betty ran off with Jamie's water gun so I don't think we can try that plan again."

Stefan and Jamie looked disappointed, I think Jamie more so because he had just been reminded of losing his gun.

"If only there was a way. What we need is some kind of -"

Reverse alarm clock were the words that I didn't finish in my sentence, because at that moment my mind suddenly exploded with information. I suddenly knew in an instant everything that would be needed to make a reverse alarm clock. The physics involved, the mathematics, the engineering, everything. It all seemed so simple, and I could probably get one rigged up in under six hours. I suddenly understood my mum when she had said, *"You will find you can achieve things normal scientists would only ever dream of."* My brain was bulging with information on this one subject, and I held my head as though I thought it might all escape through my ears.

"So this is what I was destined to do," I whispered to myself in awe.

"Are you alright, Polly?" Sara asked in concern.

"I know how we are going to get the locket! I think we can rescue Ted tonight! I need to get to my dad's cellar. I need his science lab! Don't forget to tell your dad about the sleepover! And you too, Jamie!" I announced excitedly, getting up swiftly and heading for the bedroom door. I stopped at the door briefly to say one last thing. "Let's meet outside Larry's scrapyard. It's close enough to the castle! Stefan knows where it is. At 7 ... no, 8 tonight!"

Stefan looked at me knowingly and smiled as though he had been waiting for this to happen to me, like it must have happened with my dad all those years before.

"We will be waiting for you, Polly, whenever you are ready," he said and smiled once again.

26

My mind was swirling with ideas as I burst through my front door a little while later after running most of the way home. My parents were both in the kitchen drinking a cup of tea and were surprised to see me back so soon looking red-faced and out of breath.

"Polly! Are you alright?" Mum asked, standing up from the wooden stool she was sat in.

"I ... need to ... make something ... in the cellar," I gasped.

My dad had the same knowing smile on his face that Stefan had. "Got a sudden rush of ideas you want to try out Pol? It's exhilarating ain't it?" He said. "Get a cold drink from the fridge first then I'll show you where everything is in the cellar."

I did as my dad asked and was soon following him down into the cellar with an ice-cold glass of pure orange juice. He showed me the large stone table I had already seen before and the various equipment it held. He then showed me a little side room I hadn't noticed before – the door cleverly blended in with the wall surrounding it - and inside this room were his various tool kits and a fridge full of various liquids he said could come in handy.

He asked me what I was planning, but I wanted to keep this one a secret. "Oh, nothing too spectacular. It is my first attempt after all."

My dad said he understood this perfectly and he

left me to my own devices, telling me to be careful.

When he had gone, I took off my digital watch and looked at it. It was one in the afternoon. If I got everything that was brewing inside my head correct, I could transform this ordinary, old-fashioned, yet reliable watch with built in alarm into the world's first reverse alarm clock – once it went off the person hearing it would fall instantly asleep. I could probably get the device up and running by five if I worked quickly, and so, working solely by instinct from what felt right in my head, I got to work.

My first invention was finished a little later than I was hoping, but by half six I stood by the work table in the cellar and looked at the finished article in awe. I had even added some sparkly glitter to give it a little creative flourish.

I didn't have anyone to test it on – I didn't want to try it on my parents, and I wasn't trying it on myself because I didn't know when I would wake up – so I decided I would just have to trust in my own ability and try it when the moment came.

I put my sparkly new watch back on and hid it underneath my shirt sleeve and went back upstairs to talk to my parents.

My mum and dad were surprisingly very willing to let me have a sleepover at the twins' house. I was hoping that the twins' had come up with a similar excuse for their parents about having a sleepover at my house and that our parents wouldn't get suspicious. Part of me suspected that they knew I was up to something and were allowing me to get on with it. After all, I was constantly hearing things about the two of them getting up to all sorts of adventures at my age, and I think it would only be fair if I had some adventures of my own!

They did insist though that I had something to eat before I went out again, so my mum dished out some spaghetti bolognese, which, although it was delicious, I ate hurriedly, anxious to return back to Sara and Naz and the boys.

The sun was quite low in the sky when I finally did set off to the scrapyard. I didn't run as fast heading there as I did to get home, as I was savouring the fact that the town had finally decided to come to life.

Kids where running around their gardens or along the pavements, or on bikes, shouting and screaming and having fun. There were zombies and various different monsters, and I saw for the first time the two troll kids I had heard about. They were made of a pale rock, perhaps limestone, although I'm no expert. They were lumbering around slowly, as though getting used to their heavy new legs, and passing a football across their garden to each other. I said hi as I passed and they both said hi back in very deep voices, like the rumbling of a volcano or the start of an earthquake.

I passed the sweet shop that had been closed previously and stopped at the window to look at the display of assorted delicacies along with a couple of other girls. One of the girls was short and dark green with short, curly, shockingly bright purple hair. The other was tall, extremely thin, and a pale grey in colour. She looked at me nervously then hid behind a nearby lamppost. She wasn't as skinny as the lamppost but somehow she managed to hide behind it so well that I couldn't even see her! I rubbed my eyes and squinted hard at the lamppost. If I did this I could just about see a grey outline and a pair of small black eyes peeping timidly at me from behind the post.

"Hi, I'm Abigail! Don't mind Laura there, she gets shy around strangers," the dark green girl said brightly as she looked me up and down. "She's a bogeyman, or should I say *bogeywoman*."

Laura allowed herself to be seen again and returned to her friend's side. So this is what a bogeywoman looked like! The coincidence of seeing someone similar to who I was off to rescue surprised me and I exclaimed, "Sorry for staring, but I'm off to rescue a bogeyman called Ted who is being kept locked up in a cellar!"

"A cellar, sounds nice, lots of places to hide in a cellar," Laura whispered. Her voice, though not loud seemed to rattle around in my head as though it hadn't passed through my ears first.

"You wouldn't like this cellar. There is nowhere to hide and it's guarded by a nasty banshee called Rory."

"Rory O' Neill!" Gasped Abigail. "My mum mentioned him and said to keep away from his castle. Good luck going up there! You'll need it!"

"Don't suppose you fancy helping out then?" I asked politely.

"No thanks!" Abigail said roughly and walked away from the shop, followed swiftly by Laura.

Laura's voice rattled around my head once again

as she walked away, "No place to hide, poor Ted. Hope you get him out of there."

"I'll try my best," I said to myself determinedly as I continued down the road to meet my friends.

27

Half an hour later and my friends and I had passed the wooden gate with the faded word "O' Neill" just about visible, and we stared up at the daunting castle. Although it looked very similar in design and shape to Stefan's home, it filled me with dread and a feeling that I wasn't welcome.

I led the way, wanting to give off an aura that I was confident and that the plan was a good one that couldn't possibly go wrong. I didn't feel that confident myself, but the rest of the gang followed me anyway. It wasn't much of a plan at the moment; basically it was find a way into the castle, find Rory and possibly Betty and put them to sleep, get the key and rescue Ted. We hadn't thought of a way to get into the castle yet, but it was Stefan's suggestion that we just trek up to the castle anyway and figure something out as we went. It was this that we were discussing as we were halfway up the untidy weed-filled path leading to the O' Neill castle.

"If we can find an open window then I will be able to transform into a bat and hopefully open the front door from inside," Stefan declared.

"If you ask me what chance we have," said Jamie, "We haven't a leg to stand on!" He was currently hopping on one leg as he waved his other leg in the air. The twins laughed nervously at this as the castle loomed larger and larger in front of us.

"We will probably have Betty to deal with too," I

said, always one to deliver bad news. "She won't be too happy after her banishment yesterday, and this will be too much fun for her to ignore."

"We will deal with her when we encounter her. You will have to put her to sleep, Pol." Stefan stated this matter-of-factly. "The reverse alarm clock looks amazing, by the way," he added with a smile.

"Thanks," I answered, rolling up my sleeve briefly to glance at my creation.

"When do we put in the earplugs?" Jamie asked. He had returned his leg now and was ambling slowly up the hill behind Stefan. The earplugs had been an obvious idea that I had overlooked when I was creating my reverse alarm clock. We didn't want to hear the alarm ourselves, otherwise we wouldn't get very far in our plan, and it was the twins who pointed this out. Stefan helped us here and flew as quickly as he could to his castle to bring us five pairs of blue earplugs.

"Earplugs go in just before I press the button, so keep them close by and listen for my call," I said. I patted my shirt pocket to check that my earplugs were still there and Jamie did the same with his shorts' pocket. Stefan tapped his waistcoat pocket and the twins, who had got changed out of their onesies into baggy red trousers and matching pink jumpers, had theirs in their trouser pockets.

We finally reached the top of the hill two minutes later and all was eerily quiet. The sun was sinking rapidly over the horizon and the entire front of the castle was swamped in shadow. There was a small lawn to cross and also a large oak tree to walk around before we got to the front door. It loomed over us, huge and forbidding. I tried pushing and pulling on the huge brass handle but, as we were expecting, the door was locked.

"See any open windows?" I whispered to Stefan as I scanned the walls. It was getting darker and darker and all I could see was a vast wall of grey.

"Just one near the top," Stefan replied, pointing to a dark slot in the wall, too high up for me to notice any details.

"Okay, you sure you want to do this?" I asked in an even quieter whisper.

"I'm not scared. Watch me go!" He replied. With a theatrical twirl, he jumped into the air. Halfway through the jump he had already changed into a bat and he soared up and up, soon lost to my sight against the dark walls.

"We have to wait now and hope he gets to the door unseen," I whispered to the twins and Jamie who were standing together looking around nervously.

"I don't think we should be here," Sara whispered, looking at her sister. Naz nodded and started to scratch heavily at her jumper.

"We will be okay together," I reassured them all.

"No, I mean, the full moon is coming very soon and I feel a change coming on," Sara whispered, louder and more urgently.

"Ham and jam!" I exclaimed under my breath. "It can't be helped. If you can, stay human as long as possible and try and stick with us when you change," I said, staring intently at the front door and hoping that Stefan would open it before the change happened. The twins would not be able to control their howling, and would most likely alert Rory and Betty to our presence.

Naz and Sara were both visibly shaking, trying to hold off the change happening till the last possible second. Sara whispered something to Naz and Naz spoke in a louder whisper to me, saying, "We are going to go behind that tree and undress. Don't wanna ruin our clothes when we transform."

I nodded and they both hurried over to the large oak tree and remained hidden from our sight.

We waited for one more minute and still all was silence. Two minutes passed, with still no sign of Stefan. In the third minute, two things happened instantaneously – the one I was hoping for and the one I was dreading. The twins cried out in a double howl as the sun finally set, and at the same time the door creaked open and Stefan peeped out at us!

"Quickly, inside!" I urged, ushering Jamie into the castle ahead of me. "Leave the doors wide open, the twins might follow!"

We were stood in a vast hallway very similar to one in Stefan's castle, except this one was poorly lit with perhaps just two or three candles, and the dim walls appeared to be caked in dust and dirt. Behind me the twins had transformed fully and were running hectically around the tree and across the lawn, chasing each other, tails wagging excitedly.

"Okay, where do you think Rory might be?" I asked, listening to my voice echo around the hall. It was probably too late to worry about making noise now, the howling would have been enough to alert anyone inside the castle. I rolled up my sleeve to get easier access to my watch, which was now also my reverse alarm clock.

"If this castle is anything like mine, which it seems to be from my quick fly around, he will stay in the master bedroom like I do. Follow me."

We had barely got to the first step in the hallway leading to the upper reaches of the castle when the noise I knew was going to come sooner or later erupted into my eardrums.

"Eeeeeh! Eeeeeh!" Betty shrieked, and emerged suddenly at the top of the stairs. "Thought you had got rid of me did you! Eeeeeeeeeeeeeeeh!" This wail was the loudest and longest we had heard yet; she lifted her head back and really let it erupt out of her. She darted down the stairs and stopped about five steps away so that she stood over us, her hands on her hips.

"Enjoy your time on the toilet?" Jamie asked Betty with a wide grin.

"Very funny, zombie boy! Eeeeeh!" Betty began dancing angrily on the spot again. The two wolves sauntered into the castle and sat up alertly by my side, eyes fixed on Betty.

"Earplugs?" Whispered Jamie quietly on my other side. I fingered my watch slowly and was about to agree to the earplug request, when another idea struck me instead.

"Not just yet, Jamie," I whispered back.

I remembered what I said to everyone earlier today about Betty possibly wanting to help us. She wouldn't be able to help us if she was asleep and I was willing therefore to give her a chance.

"Hi, Betty!" I said in as friendly a tone as I could muster. Betty wailed loudly in reply but I stuck with the politeness. "We thought we would come up to see if you wanted to play a game with us."

I thought she was going to shriek at me then, but instead she stared at me in puzzlement. "A game?" She asked.

"Yeah, I was thinking perhaps we could play tag. You run away and one of us can try and catch you."

Betty thought about this and started spinning around on the steps. "You would never catch me! Not a chance!" She exclaimed excitedly.

"Maybe not one of us could catch you, but maybe two could," I said. "I bet Sara and Naz could catch you if they work together!"

The twins both barked in agreement at this, their tails wagging excitedly. Betty looked at the wolves intently as though considering this prospect.

"No," she said finally and then laughed her high pitched laugh. "If we are to play this game then I want Stefan to catch me."

She looked at Stefan who smiled back at her. "If Stefan catches me, I will help you. I know why you are really here. Eeeeeh! You'll never get the key on your own! Eeeeeh!"

I didn't want Stefan to go because we needed him to guide us through the castle, but we also didn't have much choice. I really didn't want to send Betty to sleep unless it was absolutely necessary, yet if I let her follow us around we would probably get nowhere. I looked at Stefan to get his opinion and he nodded.

"Okay, Betty, I accept the challenge!" Stefan declared loudly even though the banshee was only a couple of feet away.

Betty hopped up and down happily and swung her cape around herself. "Catch me if you can!" She shouted suddenly, and with a twirl she changed into a shadow and zipped around us and out of the front door!

Stefan adjusted the collar on the shirt beneath his waistcoat and looked at me and Jamie. "Just keep going upstairs to the third floor, the master bedroom has large double doors," he said then looked out of the huge front doors. The shadow of Betty could still be seen in the moonlight hovering on the lawn, waiting to see if Stefan would start to chase her or not.

"Okay, good luck guys. Go and rescue Ted!" Stefan enthused and then, with a flourish which impressed me more every time I saw it, he transformed into a bat and flew rapidly after Betty.

28

"We didn't even ask where the cellar is to get to Ted!" Jamie said as we walked down yet another corridor, getting more and more lost as we went along.

"We haven't even found the staircase leading upwards to Rory yet, so we will worry about the cellar when we get round to it!"

I was trying not to get frustrated, but the possibility of getting lost had never occurred to us in all our planning, and we were definitely lost. We had been wandering around corridor after corridor for fifteen minutes and we hadn't found any stairs other than the ones in the main entranceway. I was also wondering why this mysterious Rory wasn't making an appearance. We were making enough noise that I continuously expected him to turn up at any second, but he never did. The twins were striding ahead of us with their noses to the cold stone floor, perhaps trying to find a scent to follow, but it seemed that they too were lost.

"Hey, Rory!" Jamie suddenly shouted. "We're here for Ted!"

I stood still to listen and to see if this shout had any effect. All was silence for perhaps ten more seconds, but then a noise slowly filtered through from above us. It was a deep and chilling sound in the gloomy stone corridor.

It was the sound of laughter.

"He knows we are here now," Jamie said

nervously.

"I think he has known all along. He is teasing us. It appears he does like having his own kind of fun after all," I replied, looking around me, feeling watched all of a sudden. The twins also appeared scared. They were huddled together and were whining, their tails no longer wagging.

The laughter stopped and it was replaced by a deep, slow voice.

"Take the next door to your right if you want the stairs going up. The door to your left leads back out of the castle if you're scared!"

"I'm *scared*, Polly," whispered Jamie. I looked around, wondering how Rory could possibly know where we were at that precise moment.

"Me too," I confessed, "But we should keep going. Don't forget we have this." I tapped the bulky watch on my wrist. It reassured us both and we took the door to the right, which sure enough, led to some stairs going upwards.

Now that we had found the stairs, the voice and the laughter had stopped and we were left in a creepy silence once more. Our feet echoed on the cold stone steps. The twins' heavy bounds, up three steps at a time, Jamie's shuffling walk and my light step all sounded a lot louder than they actually were. Even my heartbeat seemed to hammer in my ears.

We now quickly found our way towards the third floor and we were facing a long, gloomy corridor. I could just about see, at the end of this corridor, a set of double doors – what Stefan assured us would be Rory's master bedroom.

"Do you think he will be there?" Jamie asked, also looking at the double doors.

"Yes," I answered. "I think he is waiting for us. It feels like he wants us to find him. Like it's a game to him."

The twins suddenly started barking excitedly, their tales wagging together like crazy. Before I could react to this, they bolted forward and ran full pelt towards the double doors which were slowly opening inwards.

"Stop!" I screamed out towards the twins, but they didn't seem to be listening; it was as though they could hear something else that we could not. I started to run after the two werewolves, but I had no chance to catch up. Before I had even got halfway down the corridor, they had ran through the double doors and the doors had slammed shut behind them. I stopped to let Jamie catch up with me.

"Okay Jamie, put your earplugs in! I'm just gonna storm in there and put him to sleep. It looks like I'll have to send the twins to sleep too, but it will have to be done now!"

I walked determinedly towards the double doors as I put in the earplugs carefully. The sound of my footsteps disappeared – the earplugs really were very effective! When I reached the bedroom, I was expecting the doors to be locked but when I pushed them angrily, they flew open easily.

Rory was stood in front of his bed waiting for me. He was short and fat with long blonde hair, and had the widest grin on his face I had ever seen on anyone. Like

Betty he was dressed all in black, but instead of a cape he wore a long black coat that was open and trailed over the floor behind him like a long wedding dress.

I didn't notice the twins or anyone else in the room, but my focus was entirely on Rory. I didn't say anything but lifted up my arm and pressed the button on my reverse alarm clock. I stared at the banshee in front of me and waited in the silence that was surrounding me for Rory to fall asleep. He continued to grin at me and then he raised his head back – he was laughing at me.

Confused and a little scared now that the anger had faded, I pressed the button again. Jamie arrived at that moment by my side and looked around, looking equally confused that Rory wasn't already asleep. Rory's lips were moving – he was saying something I couldn't hear. He was edging closer and closer to the doorway where Jamie and I stood. I kept pressing the button, feeling frustrated that it didn't seem to be working, yet unable to think of anything else to do.

This was our only plan, everyone had put their faith in me and I was letting them down. Rory was still grinning maniacally as he edged closer and suddenly, fast as a flash, he had darted behind us. He must have clashed our heads together, because I found myself lying unconscious in a heap next to Jamie's equally unmoving body.

29

Before I opened my eyes I was aware of two feelings. The first was a thumping headache which pounded along with my heartbeat. The second was the feel of cold metal digging into my wrists. When I opened my eyes, Rory was still grinning at me. I let out a little scream and instinctively tried to move away from the grinning face, which was barely a foot away from me, and found that I couldn't move at all. The cold metal I could feel on my wrists dug into my skin as I struggled – they were shackles and I was pinned to the wall, my arms and body forming an uncomfortable "Y" shape. My legs were also chained and shackled to the wall. I swung out my foot in the hope that I could kick Rory but he was a few inches too far away and my foot swept around, just missing Rory's ankle. His grin never faltered and he continued to stand there in silence staring at me.

My earplugs must have been removed or had fell out, as I heard a groan to my right, and finally turning away from Rory, I noticed that Jamie was shackled beside me. Well, part of Jamie was shackled to the right of me, and part of him was shackled to the left of me. To my right, the majority of Jamie was strapped to the wall – a lot more securely than me too – his legs, waist and neck were all pinioned to the slimy wall so he couldn't move at all. Jamie's arms had been detached and were pulling hopelessly on their own little chains, shackled tightly around his wrists and stuck to the wall on my left hand side.

We were trapped in some kind of gloomy, wet, dripping dungeon. There was an electric light swinging from the ceiling. It didn't give off a lot of light but it illuminated a stone table I could just about see behind the large bulk that was Rory.

The grinning banshee noticed where I was looking and suddenly stepped aside. He evidently wanted me to see what he had done. My rucksack was lying on the table. It had been emptied, and the contents hadn't just been ruined – they had been destroyed! The contents of my Amaze-All-Portable-Science experiment kit had been tipped out and smashed – a colourful mixture of various potions was still dripping from the table. My voice recorder was in pieces, as was my watch which had been lately my failed reverse alarm clock. It looked like both of these devices had been smashed by a hammer.

"How … how could you?" I stuttered and burst into tears.

Rory's evil grin remained as he finally spoke. "I know what you have been planning – to steal my key and set my little captive free. Well, it's not going to happen!" Rory laughed, a deep rumbling sound that was even worse to bear than Betty's high pitched shrieking laugh. "I've been having a little fun as you can see. This is just a little warning, to tell you not to attempt to break into my castle again! If you do, well, I won't be so kind!"

Rory walked around the table which held my ruined belongings, and paused by the open doorway on the far side of the dungeon. "I might just let you out of them chains in the morning. I'll let you get soaked on those damp walls for a bit first!"

Before I could react to any of this, Rory had stormed out of the room, slamming the very sturdy looking door behind him. His laughter seemed to remain behind for several seconds like a bad lingering smell before disappearing to follow its owner.

I sniffed, unable to wipe the tears that had fell onto my cheeks. Jamie groaned again and mumbled something I couldn't quite make out.

"What was that, Jamie?" I sniffed again.

"I said I told you we didn't have a leg to stand on!" Jamie giggled weakly then coughed.

I wanted to cuddle him but couldn't. My arms were getting really tired and the metal shackles were really stinging. We were in quite a predicament here – imprisoned in a dungeon probably in a remote and hidden part of an evil banshee's castle, and it was all my fault.

As though he had read my mind or could tell what I was feeling at that moment, Jamie said, "Don't blame yourself, Polly. We all wanted to help."

I smiled at Jamie, grateful for his kind words. "I know it's too late now, but I think I know why the reverse alarm clock didn't work," I said eventually.

"What went wrong?" Jamie asked kindly.

"I didn't set the alarm. An alarm can't go off unless you set it first." I sighed. "Oh well, too late now."

"Don't worry," Jamie encouraged. "Stefan will help us. Mark my words, he's a legend that guy!"

I wanted to share in Jamie's enthusiasm but I couldn't see how he could help us. How was he going to get rid of both Betty and Rory and manage to find us in this gloomy dungeon? I wondered then if there was someone else who could possibly help us.

"Well Mum," I said loudly to the dark, grim dungeon, "I know I said not to turn invisible and follow me, but if you are here right now, we would appreciate some help!"

I waited and listened expectantly. There was no reply and my mum failed to materialise. I felt strangely disappointed that she had actually listened to me yesterday and had not followed me.

"Oh, no," whispered Jamie suddenly.

"What is it?" I asked, concerned.

"Can't you hear it?"

At first I couldn't hear anything other than the drip–drip of water and mud from somewhere on the ceiling, but then a noise we were all too familiar with drifted slowly towards us and it was getting louder.

"Eeeeeh! Eeeeeh!"

Just when I thought things couldn't get any worse. Betty was coming to add to the mischief.

30

"Don't let her get to you, Jamie. Don't say anything. She thrives off the attention," I urged as Jamie began to mumble nervously.

"Don't let her take my hands again!" Jamie pleaded.

"I won't let her," I reassured Jamie as the shrieking reached an unbearable crescendo. Betty suddenly pushed the dungeon door open and stood in the doorway with a big smile on her face.

I didn't say anything. Although he was struggling to stay composed, Jamie remained silent too.

"Betty's here!" The banshee announced dramatically then burst into little dance. She suddenly started to recite a little poem in a sing-song voice:

"Betty is here for all to see,
Betty is dancing and Betty is free."

"Please don't rub it in, Betty," I urged, unable to listen to my own advice and remain quiet. Betty continued with her recital, dancing happily.

"Betty can see you're in a tight spot,
So Betty will have to pick the lock!"

I was about to shout at Betty to shut up, before I realised what it was that she had just said.

"Eh?" I asked.
Betty continued with her poem unperturbed.

"Betty can help you and set you free,
Stefan helped me, so I will help he,
Let's do it quickly, one, two, three,
Then all we need is to get Ted's key!"

Before I could react to anything that Betty had just said, she had produced a paper clip from one of her pockets and was busy unshackling Jamie's arms. Moving at lightning speed, she hastily moved on to Jamie's legs and then his neck. Jamie was quickly freed and his detached arms shuffled back to the zombie to be reattached.

"Hey, thanks Betty!" Exclaimed Jamie gratefully to Betty who had moved on to releasing me from my chains.

"Eeeeeh! No prob!" She shrieked in reply.

"Yeah, thanks Betty," I said sincerely, as I too was freed from the shackles. I twisted my wrists round painfully, wondering if anything was broken. I wondered what had happened to Betty. I had a feeling that she might have been willing to help us a little, but I wasn't expecting her to be so friendly about it. *What had Stefan done to make her react like this?*

"Where's Stefan?" Asked Jamie, echoing my thoughts.

Betty started dancing around happily once again.

"You'll see! Follow me!" She exclaimed excitedly. "Follow me! Follow me!" She urged.

We didn't really have any other choice, but I wasn't going to leave without collecting my belongings first. I picked up my empty rucksack and I brushed the remains of my watch and my voice recorder into the bag. Maybe I could salvage something from them when I eventually got home. The potions and the rest of my Amaze-All-Portable-Science experiment kit that I had yet to make use of were now totally destroyed, so sadly I left them on the table.

"Follow me!" Betty urged again impatiently. Intrigued as to what we might find, we followed the hyperactive banshee out of the dungeon door and along a seemingly endless labyrinth of gloomy, mouldy corridors. If we had attempted to make our way out on our own, we would have probably been stuck down here and lost forever.

"Where's Rory?" I asked on one of the rare occasions when Betty paused to let us catch up with her.

"You'll see! You'll see! Listen carefully!" Betty chanted, and when she finally calmed down, I tried to listen carefully as we walked down yet another corridor. There was a deep rumbling noise, which, as we got closer became a voice in distress, and as we got closer still I could make out words repeated incessantly.

"Get off me! Let me go! Get off me!" In-between the words were deep growls and screams. Something was happening to Rory and he wasn't very happy about it!

What was going on? Had Stefan done something to Rory, or was it perhaps the twins?

Rory's shouting had become unbearably loud now

as Betty stopped at a long staircase. "Just up there. Come on!"

She was already bounding up the steep stairs two at a time. I followed at a slower pace, followed shortly by Jamie, who had pulled his hands out once again to use as earplugs against Rory's loud protestations.

I helped Jamie up the last few steps, and as we pushed open the door at the top, we saw together what was bothering Rory. We found ourselves back in the main hallway close to the stairway and opposite the front door. Rory was being pinned to the wall to our left. He wasn't being pinned by Stefan or the twins, but by an invisible force. I knew by the breeze in the room and the candles flickering above my head what the invisible force was immediately.

"Loretta!" I gasped excitedly.

Betty was now standing to the left of her trapped uncle, and to his right stood Stefan. The vampire noticed me and Jamie stood in the doorway and beckoned us over to him. He was waving something shiny and golden in his hands – Rory's locket!

"Hey Pol! Hey Jamie!" He called out as we got closer.

"You have been busy!" I shouted out and laughed. I had to shout to be heard over Rory, who seemed to be getting noisier and angrier.

"Not quite done yet!" Stefan yelled, pointing to the locket. "Let's get this done with!"

Betty opened a door close to where Rory was pinned to the wall, and we all followed her, relieved to be out of the breeze and a little shielded from the noise.

"How long can Loretta hold Rory like that?" I asked, concerned. I didn't want to be around when Rory was finally released from the wall.

"Long enough for us to be far gone from here!" Stefan said, reassuring me as though he knew what I was thinking.

"And where are the twins?" I asked, suddenly aware of their absence. I hadn't seen them since they ran into Rory's bedroom ahead of me.

"It seems they had been given some drugged dog food." Stefan explained. "I've left them to sleep it off in one of the cloakrooms. I've left their clothes nearby too, just in case they transform back."

Stefan must have seen my worried look because he added, "Don't worry, we will wake them up before we leave!"

We were heading down a long staircase and Rory's bellowing was quickly fading as we descended. Instead there was another noise coming up from below us. It was the sound of sobbing, which seemed to come straight into my head in a way that I had heard a few hours back, outside the sweet shop.

"I think I can hear Ted!" I gasped.

It seemed that the others could hear him too. Stefan rubbed his ears as though confused at the way the noise seemed to get straight into his head without passing anywhere else. Even Jamie had let his hands return back onto his arms so he could give his ears a good itch.

"Eeeeeh! Just here!" Betty declared, stopping at a plain wooden door at the bottom of the staircase.

Stefan rummaged in his waistcoat pocket and pulled out the golden locket. He opened it easily and tried the plain looking iron key that was inside the locket in the lock and it slid in smoothly.

"Okay," he whispered, and opened the cellar door that was Ted's prison.

31

The room was brightly lit and completely bare of any furnishings. A grey bundle was slumped in one corner. The grey bundle untangled itself when the door opened, and a head peeped out from between long skinny grey legs. Ted looked up at us with the saddest eyes I had ever seen. They were like the eyes of a misbehaving puppy trying to plead to its master that it hadn't done anything wrong – *the sofa had always been ripped with the stuffing thrown all around the carpet.*

"Go away," Ted pleaded dejectedly. His voiced echoed around my skull sadly. Betty appeared in the doorway and Ted hid his face once again between his legs. If I didn't already know Ted was there, he could easily have been mistaken for a pile of rags in the corner – it was like an optical illusion.

"Please leave me alone," Ted whined. Betty looked down at her feet in shame.

"I'm sorry, Ted," she mumbled. Ted looked up with tears in his eyes, the optical illusion of the pile of rags in the corner vanishing once again.

"What did you say?" He asked, his voice sounding a little brighter than before.

"You are free to go Ted. I'm sorry," Betty said clearly, and let out a little high pitched whine as she continued to stare at her feet. I don't know what Stefan had said to her to make her react like this, but I felt that Betty was genuinely ashamed of her cruel actions towards Ted.

I didn't know what to say to a bogeyman, but I thought I should say something. "Betty is a changed girl, she won't be cruel anymore."

I looked up at Betty and she smiled warmly at me.

"Can I still leave?" Ted asked shyly, not wanting to look at Betty.

"You can stay at my house if you have nowhere else, Ted," Jamie suggested cheerfully, then added in a moment of inspiration, "There's some nice cupboards to hide in!"

Ted suddenly stood up. He was quite tall, grey, and very skinny. He was wearing what appeared to be a darker grey sack in the style of a nightgown. His grey knobbly knees protruded out from the bottom of the sack nightgown.

"And a bed to hide under too?" He asked, sounding hopeful.

"It's a bit cramped and dark under there I'm afraid," Jamie said with a grin.

"Just the way I like it!" Ted exclaimed, and his face lit up with a big smile. "Dark and cramped with lots of shadows, and people to scare!"

"I bet you could scare my dad!" Jamie suggested excitedly and Ted clapped his hands with joy at the idea.

"I can *really* go now? You really don't mind?" Ted asked nervously, looking from Betty to me, and then to Jamie and Stefan. Betty stood aside from the door graciously and we all did the same.

"You can go now, Teddy. I'm sorry," Betty said meekly.

"And you're more than welcome at my house, Ted!" Jamie cried. "We won't tell Dad, it'll be a scary surprise!"

"I like the sound of that!" Ted said eagerly. He took a step towards the cellar door and then dashed through it onto the staircase outside quickly, as though we were going to change our mind and decide to keep him locked up.

Now that he was stood in a dark and gloomy passageway, it was really difficult to see him; he blended in so well with the grimy walls that it was spooky.

"Job done!" Stefan suddenly cried out as we all bustled onto the staircase and began to climb back up them. "Shall we head off back home now?"

I looked round at the gang of us five tired looking kids and sighed with relief. "I think we are all ready for our beds. It has been another long day!"

Rory was still shouting at the top of his lungs when we finally emerged into the main hall again. Loretta wasn't yet showing any signs of tiring in keeping Rory at bay either. Rory spotted Ted as he peeped nervously from the door and he screamed, a deep, rumbling roar that shook the floor. A dusty candlestick holder fell from its perch on the wall.

"Get back in the cellar, you!" Rory roared.

For one moment I thought Ted would obey and run back downstairs, but instead he scurried across the room towards the vast front doors, which were still standing wide open. He ran outside and I could just make out his dark figure scurrying to hide behind the large oak tree on the lawn.

"Grrrrrraah!" Rory rumbled again in anger and frustration.

"I think you should go. Eeeeh!" Betty suggested, as she looked nervously at her uncle. She hadn't shrieked as much in the past half an hour or so, and I looked at her admiringly. I wondered again what had happened to make her have a sudden change in heart, because she was really trying to be friendly with us, and it must have been hard for her to turn away from her natural banshee-like ways and to really help us.

"Thanks again, Betty," I said earnestly. "You should come down from the castle and see us again sometime. I don't think it would be safe for us to come up here again though!" I said and laughed nervously.

Betty glanced again at Rory, who had gone quieter than usual – he was now making a low moaning noise and grumbling to himself. "I'll say hi sometime. The twins are back!"

Betty suddenly pointed to a small door to the left of the front door where Naz and Sara, in human form and once again wearing the clothes they came up the hill in, staggered towards us, rubbing their eyes. They looked apprehensively at Rory, seemingly held to the wall by nothing, and stopped by the front door.

"What have we missed?" They both asked together.

"Oh, not much. Just Betty and Loretta helping us rescue Ted!" I exclaimed, and their reaction to this was priceless! I knew they had a million questions to ask me at that moment but I silenced them with my hand. "Let's get out of here first! I'm getting more and more nervous being this close to Rory!"

We all walked over to the front door. Stefan came last, pausing to talk to Loretta and asking the poltergeist to hold onto Rory for about half an hour longer and then to hurry on back home. I wouldn't want to be around when Rory was finally released, and I asked Stefan what would happen.

"Oh, he will trash his castle no doubt. He won't go beyond his castle grounds though, so we're quite safe once we pass the gate at the bottom of the hill."

"Why won't he go past there?" I asked, intrigued.

"That's a long tale for another day!" Stefan said and laughed.

I think I recognised the cheeky little glint in his eye then, so I asked, "Something to do with you and my dad perhaps?"

"Perhaps," he said with a smile, but would say no more about it.

"What about you, Betty?" I asked. Betty was stood in the doorway with her hands on her hips. "What will Rory do to you?"

"He won't catch me! Eeeeeh!" Betty shrieked. "He's tried many times, I'm far too fast!"

"If you ever want to come and stay with me …" I began, but Betty interrupted me.

"No, I'm happy to stay here," she insisted. "I think you should go now before Loretta gets too tired!"

We all made our goodbyes to Betty, and shouted farewell to Loretta, and even Ted sneaked out nervously from behind his tree to wave goodbye to Betty. We finally made our way back down the hill, Ted and Jamie taking the lead, walking slowly and carefully under the cloudy and currently moonless night sky.

32

From walking down the hill of one castle, we found ourselves walking up the hill to another. Although Jamie and I were supposed to be having a sleepover at the twin's home, the twins were supposed to be having a sleepover at my house, so we found that we had nowhere to stay. Stefan offered to let us have a couple of rooms in his castle for the night, so we took our time labouring up the steep winding path to his home.

We should have told our parents we were planning a sleepover here in the first place. It would have saved a lot of worrying about whether our little lie would get found out! Jamie and Ted had took the lead, talking animatedly together as though they were already best friends. The twins were at the back, talking together, and I walked with Stefan, trying to keep up with his long strides.

There was one nagging question on my mind that I really needed answering, so I asked it Stefan now.

"How on Earth did you catch Betty, and what did you say to her that made her suddenly so friendly?"

"Well, let's get to the castle and I'll tell you all around the sofa before we go to bed," Stefan answered with a yawn.

I was very tired myself but I felt awake enough for one more quick chat amongst my friends.

"And what about you two?" I addressed the twins who were dawdling along behind me. "Why did you both suddenly run off towards Rory's room like you did? Was it the smell of the drugged dog food?"

The twins grinned at this, but both shook their head.

"It was the whistle. Did you not hear it?" Sara asked me, looking perplexed.

I shook my head. "Must have been a dog whistle! You are gonna have to try and control these animal urges. We could have been in trouble back there!" I said, then smiled at the twins.

We had almost got to the end of the path leading up the hill when an almighty roar erupted from behind us, coming from the castle we had just left. Rory had finally been set free and from the sound of it, he was rampaging around his castle and screaming.

"Here comes Loretta!" Jamie cried and pointed to the bottom of the hill where the gate had swung open. I could see the grass on the hill parting as Loretta stormed along at hurricane speed, and when the breeze hit us a couple of seconds later, it knocked us all off our feet!

"She forgets her own strength sometimes!" Stefan said as he sat up and rubbed his elbows.

The breeze circled us all a couple of times like a sheepdog rounding up its herd of sheep, and then the front door of the castle burst open as Loretta whizzed off for a much deserved rest, wherever it was that she went to sleep.

"Let's go then, I think hot chocolates may be needed all round!" Stefan declared to a cheer of approval.

The chocolate was prepared in double quick time and we were soon settled around the sofas in the room in which we had performed the banishment charm, which now seemed like a very long time ago.

Even Rhubarb the bright red lobster was placed on a sofa with a plate of hot chocolate to sip on, which Jamie and Ted thought was hilarious.

"Well everyone," Stefan announced as we all finally got cosy with our hot drinks. "There's just one little bit to tell, because I bet you are all wondering what happened with Betty today after I agreed to chase her!"

I nodded eagerly and Jamie looked up from watching Rhubarb with interest.

"She was being very nice, wasn't she?" Jamie pondered.

"Yes, people can surprise you sometimes," Stefan began. "I guess her reaction surprised me too, but I'm getting ahead of myself here. First there was the chase!"

Jamie clapped his hands in excitement and we all listened attentively as Stefan told us of his chase with Betty, and what happened afterwards.

"I knew I would never be able to catch Betty in an out and out race. If she had offered to race me instead of playing tag, she would have won easily. As it was, I knew that she would keep stopping to let me catch up and make sure I was still playing the game how she wanted it to go.

"I humoured her for a little while and made sure that she could see me labouring to keep up. I said things like, *"You're too fast, Betty,"* just to keep her happy.

After about ten minutes of this I got bored and I simply hid when I knew she wasn't looking! As I knew she would do, Betty returned back to the spot where she had saw me last, which just happened to be just outside my own gate at the bottom of the hill. I pounced on her then. It really was that simple!

"She struggled and shrieked and complained that I cheated, but eventually she calmed down and then she asked me what I wanted."

Stefan paused here to take a gulp of his hot chocolate.

"You asked her to help rescue Ted?" Sara suggested.

"No, I didn't do that," Stefan said.

"You told her to be nice or we will give her the runs again!" Jamie cried out and giggled.

"No, but that would have been a funny idea, Jamie!" Stefan replied.

"Go on then, what did you do?" I asked, intrigued.

"Well," said Stefan slowly, seemingly enjoying the suspense he was building up around the sofa. "I asked Betty to apologise to Loretta!"

"Eh?" I said.

"Yeah. I told Betty that I forgave her for terrorizing Loretta the other day, and that the banishment charm would be lifted from the castle, as long as she apologised to Loretta."

"And after that she suddenly became really friendly?" I asked, curious.

Stefan nodded slowly. "I guess forgiveness is a

powerful and mysterious force to be reckoned with. She seemed really touched that I had offered to remove the banishment charm. I had been hoping that Betty and Loretta could become friends, so I could get Loretta down to the castle to help you guys, and the plan worked better than I hoped, as you lot saw!"

"And you made Betty a nicer person in the process!" I said and then added thoughtfully, "I wonder if it will last, though? Being around Rory all day can't help."

Stefan looked into his mug reflectively as he thought about this. "I think she will be nicer and friendlier around us, but she is always going to have that mischievous side."

"Which I think we all love a little bit really," I added.

Everybody nodded, and Rhubarb said *"Glub,"* which made us all burst out laughing.

"I think on that reflective note, it's bedtime, guys!" Stefan announced as he picked up his pet lobster to return him to his tank.

We all agreed to this proposal, and after being one by one shown to our separate bedrooms, I leapt onto my bed. It was a large double bed all to myself, and I spread myself out and relaxed. I don't know about my friends in the other rooms, but I was soundly asleep less than a minute later.

33

The following day was a lazy and pretty uneventful day, until the evening, when my parents sat me down in the living room and asked me a very important question.

Before I get to that question however, I should probably quickly tell you what I did in this lazy and uneventful day.

I must have woke up around midday – the sun was shining brightly through a narrow window directly into my eyes. My friends were all up and talking in the lounge area we had chatted in last night when I finally dragged myself out of the comfortable bed. After a quick breakfast of cereal we decided to head off back home. Stefan walked with us to the bottom of his hill and said farewell to us at the gate.

"It's been quite an adventure, Polly," he said to me cheerfully after saying goodbye to the twins and Jamie. He had gave Jamie back his toy water gun which Betty had returned to Stefan sometime last night. "I hope it will be the first of many adventures."

There was something in the way he said this that made me look at him curiously then. Of course it would be the first of many adventures, why would he say that? I hugged Stefan and promised to be up to see him again tomorrow, then the rest of us headed back home.

We parted with the twins first as their home was closest, walking with them to the gate of their front garden.

"See ya tomorrow!" I said to the twins as we hugged one another.

"You better! We haven't saw your house yet!" Sara cried out.

There was just Ted, Jamie and I left now, and we headed back to our street happily. Ted darted from lamppost to lamppost as though he was nervous to be seen out in the sunshine. Jamie occasionally pulled off his head and rolled it down the street ahead of him, giggling as he popped his head back on with his hair all covered in dust. I sauntered along, thinking of the hectic past few days I had just gone through. I had only found out I was moving house on Sunday and given how much had happened to me and my friends between then and now, I could hardly believe it was now only Thursday!

Because I no longer had a watch that worked, I had no idea what time I got home at, but I guessed it was around three. I said farewell to Jamie and Ted at their front door and shook Jamie's hand. It came unattached as I held it and Jamie laughed at this. I joined in with the laughter, but quickly handed the hand back to Jamie. Ted had already found a bush beneath the window to hide behind. He seemed so much happier now, and I hoped that Jamie's dad would be happy to let him stay. Ted and Jamie had been making plans together on how they were going to scare Terry all afternoon, so I hoped he would see the funny side of it when he did find out he had a bogeyman hiding under his son's bed!

When I got home, my mum was in the living room

watching the television. It seemed that even in the mysterious town of Wolfwich, with no phone signal, Mum's favourite TV show still aired. She greeted me friendlily and asked how the sleepover at the twins' went.

I decided then that I would tell Mum some of the truth. I told her we had decided on a sleepover at the castle instead. I didn't tell her about being shackled in a dungeon for a lot of last night in the O' Neill Castle, however. I thought Mum might have been angry with me, but she smiled and said, "I'm glad you told the truth, Polly."

I thought this was a bit of an unusual response from her, but I put it under the *"unusual things that parents say"* category and went to say hi to Dad. Dad was busy in his workshop / laboratory fiddling with what looked like a new brand of mobile phone.

"Is that for work, or something for the scientist part of you?" I asked my dad cheekily after sneaking up on him.

"Oh, hi Pol! This is work I'm afraid. Some of my own ideas are probably beyond the ideas in current technology, so that would be cheating!" Dad stared at me intently. I hoped he couldn't see the bruises on my wrists from the shackles that I found myself in last night.

"How did your science experiment go? Did it work alright?" He asked finally.

"Oh, I'm afraid it broke," I admitted shyly.

"It broke?" Dad asked, perplexed.

"I forgot to set it correctly," I admitted.

Dad chuckled at this and nodded. Remembering

to set things correctly was a common problem, it seemed. I decided then to tell Dad a little bit more than I had told Mum.

"Don't tell Mum, but I had a little bit of trouble with Rory!" I whispered.

Dad's big bushy grey eyebrows raised. "Rory? The banshee Rory who lives in the castle up there?"

I nodded shyly.

"You had a brush with Rory and you came back unscathed to tell the tale! Very impressive Pol!"

I pulled my shirt sleeves further down over my wrists nervously as Dad chuckled. He continued with his work without asking any more questions, which was another very unusual response from my dad. I think I must have the most unusual parents in the world, and not just because one can become invisible and the other is a mad scientist!

I left my dad to get on with his work and I spent the rest of the afternoon in the bath.

In the evening, my parents both came to my room where I was sat reading a book, feeling refreshed and actually thankful to have my first relaxed day since arriving at Wolfwich.

"Get your shoes on Polly," my dad stated sternly. "We are off for a drive to the twins' house. There is something important we have to discuss!"

I looked from one parent to the other nervously. What could this be about? Had Dad told Mum about what I had said about Rory, and were we all about to be told off? What my mum said next seemed to confirm this in my eyes.

"Jamie and his dad are already there, we are running a bit late, so hurry up!"

Five minutes later, I was sat in the car nervously. Would we all get a massive telling off for doing so many things without telling anyone where we were going?

It wasn't long before I got to find out, because another five minutes later and I was sat in the twins' living room with Jamie, Naz, Sara, Stefan, and five stern looking parents. My dad was the first to break the awkward silence, and he gave a little speech, and then asked the very important question, and it wasn't what I was expecting.

34

"So kids, we have all been here since Monday, and I bet these past few days have been very eventful and informative for all of you!" Dad began, looking around at us all strictly over his glasses. "You have all gone through changes, some more dramatic than others, and you have all discovered more about yourselves. We as your parents all went through this ourselves, ooh, thirty years ago now!" The parents all chuckled and looked embarrassed at this – they didn't want to be reminded of how many years had passed.

"Thirty years ago, we had some interesting times in our first week here in Wolfwich too!" More chuckles from the adults here as they thought back to whatever adventures they must have had. "And thirty years ago, our parents sat us all down and asked us the same question I am going to ask you now."

I sat up in apprehension of what Dad was about to ask. Jamie, Sara and Naz did the same. Stefan was sat back, relaxed. He must have already heard this question alongside my dad all those years ago – another secret that Stefan had kept from me.

"The question is a simple one. Do you want to continue to live in Wolfwich, or do you want to return to a more ordinary life like you were living this time last week?"

I think the four of us who hadn't heard this question before gasped; it was a little unexpected.

"Will I still be a zombie?" Jamie asked simply.

Jamie's dad answered. "No, son, you will return to being a normal everyday kid, and I'll stop being a zombie too. I'm happy either way so it's down to you, Jamie."

"And that's the same for us all," Dad said. "Sara and Naz, you will no longer be werewolves, along with Anita and Rav. Polly, you will still love science and be very gifted at it, but you won't feel that sudden surge of knowledge and inspiration as easily as you did yesterday, and your mum will not be able to turn invisible again."

I looked at Jamie and the twins thoughtfully. I hoped that they felt the same way that I did – I really wanted to stay.

My mum spoke up then, giving us a little bit more to think about. "We will let you all think it through on your own in a moment, but first I think you should all know that thirty years ago we said no when asked this question."

There was a murmur of shock at this announcement, and my mum continued. "We were given a couple of weeks to stay in Wolfwich rather than a few days like yourselves so maybe that made a difference, I don't know. Some of us, like Larry, and Stefan, and his brother Viktor, wanted to stay. The rest of us decided that although we had had a great, if not unusual time, and made some brilliant, irreplaceable friends, we wanted to return to some kind of normality.

"We still had happy lives, and we still kept in touch, and we raised families of our own. The decision however is entirely yours. In fact, it is because of you children that we decided to return."

My mum stopped here to take a few breaths and see how everyone was reacting to the decision we had to make. I tried to judge how everyone in the room was thinking, but I just couldn't do it.

My mum continued to speak, explaining why they had decided to return to Wolfwich. "I don't know if Stefan or anyone else has mentioned this to you, but kids regularly turn up here with their parents every ten years on the first few days of the summer holidays. It is often called the *Day of Change.*"

Stefan nodded at this. I vaguely remembered Stefan mentioning something about the Day of Change shortly after meeting him for the first time. Mum continued with her tale, slowly but confidently like a school teacher.

"After the first week, or even the first month, kids come and then some stay and some return to their original lives. The ones that do stay often keep in touch with the ones that leave for many, many years. When the ones that stay learn that some of their friends have started a family of their own, there generally comes a letter, usually when the child is around ten to thirteen years old, asking whether the parents would like their child to come and live in the mysterious little town of Wolfwich. A lot of people ignore the letter, but for some, the call to return to this mysterious little town is too strong, and they think it would be a good learning experience for their child to discover their real selves.

"It was Stefan here who wrote to us regularly, and

all of us adults in this room replied that it was our duty to return."

My mum paused to look around at us all again. Stefan blushed as he realised everyone in the room was staring at him. *So it was because of Stefan that I had moved to Wolfwich with my two best friends and had all these crazy adventures!*

"I'll be honest with you," Mum said as everyone's eyes returned to her. "I've been looking forward to coming back for many, many years, ever since Polly was born!"

I felt tears coming in my eyes at this, but I held them back and smiled at my mother.

"I think we should leave you to make a decision," my dad said. "Remember though, it's an individual choice, not a group one, so decide what you feel in your heart."

The adults left the room then and left us to make the most important decision we have ever had to make.

For me the decision was easy, and as it turned out, everyone was very quick to make up their minds.

"I feel like I belong here," I declared, speaking up first after our parents had left. "For me, I'm staying."

The twins were whispering to each other, and soon Naz spoke up for both of them. "We have never felt so free as we felt when we were wolves, so simply, we are staying!"

We all looked at Stefan now to see what he had to say. "Well, you all know that I made the decision to stay here all those years ago, and you could say I'm responsible for bringing you all here, so my decision is still the same as it was back then. I'm staying!"

Jamie cheered at this and the twins applauded. I was thinking about Stefan's twin brother, Viktor, and his parents. Where were they? I was sure that I had asked him this once, but that was just before Betty's first arrival and I had forgotten about it since then. I considered asking Stefan this now, but decided against it. Everybody was looking so happy, and I didn't know what kind of answer I was going to get from that question.

It was now Jamie's turn to decide, and he was as determined as the rest of us in his answer.

"I can't leave Ted on his own now that we have just rescued him, and I've made the most amazing friends here in this room, so I'm staying!" Jamie ran over to each of us in turn and hugged us tightly. "Why is Ted not here anyway?" Jamie asked. "Does he not get to choose if he wants to return home?"

Stefan shook his head sadly. "There are some magical creatures here that don't come from what you would call the *"real world"*. They drift here from all over the magical lands around the world because they feel like they belong here. Ted was one of those. Betty and Rory were too, actually!"

"I belong here too," Jamie said firmly.

"And me," the twins called out together.

"Together forever," I declared.

"Together forever!" Jamie, Stefan and the twins echoed my statement and we all put our hands together.

"We are gonna have some fun together!" Jamie cried out excitedly and he jumped up and down on the spot.

"We sure are, Jamie! Starting with giving your dad a real good scare when he returns home and sees Ted!" I said happily.

"It will be epic!" Jamie shouted as he continued to jump up and down.

"What would really make it awesome is if we had a -"

My brain was pelted by a surge of information as different ideas flowed through my brain about the suggestion I was going to make. Numbers and technology and mechanics all flowed through me and I clapped my hands excitedly. In Jamie's words, this idea was indeed going to be *epic.*

Indeed, it promised to be a very interesting summer.

THE END

The Story continues in …

Polly Peartree and the Vampire's Curse

Read on for the opening two chapters …

1

"Oh, ham and jam!" I exclaimed in frustration. I had adopted my father's phrase as my own in the two weeks or so that had passed since our move to the mysterious little town of Wolfwich was made permanent. It had been a hectic couple of weeks that was for sure, and also one of the most creative periods I have ever experienced. I must have created a dozen different gadgets and potions in those two weeks, and it all began on the evening that Jamie, my zombie friend and next door neighbour had decided he wanted to scare his dad, with the help of his new bogeyman friend, Ted.

If any of you are wondering why I am making potions and creating gadgets and hanging around with zombies, then maybe I should give a little recap on who I am. My name is Polly Patricia Peartree, I am eleven years old, and I found out very recently that I come from a long line of mad scientists (that is my dad's term, not mine - I'm not really that crazy!) I found this out when I moved to the magical town of Wolfwich, along with my identical twin best friends, Naz and Sara, and a boy I recognised from school called Jamie. I soon found out, to my amazement, that the twins were actually werewolves and Jamie had become a zombie! Along with a friend we made called Stefan, who was a vampire who had lived in Wolfwich for thirty years but had barely aged and still looked twelve, we had a few adventures in that first week, involving banshees, poltergeists, and even a talking lobster!

We had moved on Monday, yet by Thursday we had been given an ultimatum by our parents – do we make the move to Wolfwich permanent and keep our unusual new-found identities, or do we return to what we would have to call a *"normal"* life back in our old hometown? It had been a simple decision in the end and we had all agreed that we were going to stay in Wolfwich.

It was on that very evening when this enormous decision had been made that I came up with my first great idea that was to kick-start my two week creation binge. It had been a simple idea. In order to really give Jamie's dad a really good scare, what we needed was a bit of atmosphere, maybe a lot of fog and some mysterious lights coming from Jamie's bedroom, which his dad would be keen to investigate. It would then have been a perfect time for Ted to jump out from under the bed and scare Jamie's dad. Ted was a bogeyman, and bogeymen like to hide, and they love it even more to jump out and scare people.

We had rescued Ted the other night from a castle he was being imprisoned in by the evil banshee, Rory. We were hoping that Jamie's dad would let him stay with them, but first we wanted to scare him!

Once I had come up with the idea of a fog and light machine, my brain was automatically filled with information on how I could make such a device. This was one of the perks I discovered about being a mad scientist living in the magical town of Wolfwich – once an idea arrived in my head, I had full knowledge on how to go about creating it.

On this occasion, the fog and light machine worked wonderfully. This was a relief as my first and only other attempt at creating something after an inspirational surge of information – a reverse alarm clock to send people to sleep instantly – failed as I forgot to set it correctly beforehand.

Terry nearly jumped out of his skin when Jamie tried out our creation the evening after its creation. I was invited for tea on that evening and Jamie had been struggling to keep a straight face when the fog started to crawl down the stairs towards the dining table where we were all sat.

When we followed Terry up the stairs, wading through the thick fog, Jamie could hardly keep himself from giggling as he saw the flashing green and yellow lights from under his bedroom door where the fog was also seeping from. When Terry opened the door and was faced with fierce red eyes and long grey arms reaching out for him, he let out a little scream and went from dark green to very pale green (he was also a zombie like his son)!

It had been a hilarious moment, and only Jamie's shrieks of laughter and the fact that Ted had ran off to hide back under the bed again calmed Terry down. He eventually saw the funny side of it and let Ted stay, which we had been hoping would happen.

After this first bit of creative success, the ideas continued to flow. In the next ten days, I remade my reverse alarm clock, tweaking it a little so that it wouldn't need setting beforehand. I soon ditched this watch after wearing it for a few days however. After winding my parents and friends up by giving them ten minute naps unexpectedly, I soon got bored of it and found it too bulky to wear. I had also created two special devices which I called the Message Boxes. These allowed the twins and myself to share text messages, even without a phone signal (the one downside to living in Wolfwich – no phones to be found anywhere!)

As well as this, I created a potion for Jamie which made his breath glow in the dark for a full three nights! I had also made Betty some special running shoes, which were lighter than air, and would mean she could run around just above the ground at a very high speed. Betty was a banshee. She had the ability to turn into a shadow and zip around wherever she pleased in shadow form. With these boots, she would be able to zip through the air in human form too!

Although Betty was very annoying and could be mischievous (she lived with her evil Uncle Rory, but luckily she didn't take after him too much), she had helped us greatly in rescuing Ted and I thought the shoes would make a brilliant gift for her.

I hadn't seen Betty since parting from her on the night Ted was rescued, but I had discovered a few days later that Wolfwich had an occasional postal service, and so I had sent her the shoes in a large parcel. That was two days ago and I had yet to hear anything from Betty, but I was hoping that she would make an appearance soon. It sounded daft in my own head, but I was sort of missing her annoying shriek!

Thinking of Betty brought me back to the present and my current creative task in hand. I had just exclaimed my new favourite expression for perhaps the third time that afternoon; I was getting frustrated as I couldn't quite get the correct measurements for my latest potion. This potion was my most ambitious undertaking yet. It was a potion very much inspired by the time that Stefan had got Loretta the poltergeist's help to banish Betty from his castle. There are two castles in Wolfwich by the way, one owned by Rory, the other by our friend, Stefan. Back then, Loretta had manipulated Stefan's pet lobster, Rhubarb, and made him talk. I was planning on doing something similar. I was going to make a potion that would make any animal that drank it more human.

2

My dad came into the lab that we now shared; him for his job as an inventor and me for my creations. He came with a hot cup of tea and a plate of biscuits and asked me how I was doing. I told him that I was getting frustrated and that I couldn't quite get the levels of the various ingredients exactly as how I saw them in my mind yesterday when I started the potion.

Dad looked at me over his red reading glasses quizzically. He had wild, bushy hair which I had noticed was getting greyer and thinner as the weeks passed. If ever there was someone who did indeed look like a mad scientist, it was my dad!

"I did say a few days ago, Polly, that maybe you are going a bit overboard with the inventions. You don't have to create them all at once, you know!" My dad looked at me with concern, then passed me a biscuit – a double choc chip cookie, one of my favourites. "Take a break for a bit, Pol. Mum is starting to forget what you look like!" Dad added and chuckled.

I guess I had been down in the lab a lot lately, so reluctantly, I followed my dad back upstairs. Mum was sat in the kitchen, dipping some chunky bread into a bowl of steaming soup. It looked and smelled delicious and my mum got up and poured me some from a huge pan before I even had to ask.

"What's the latest creation, Pol?" Mum asked as I sat down at the table in front of my steaming bowl of chicken and celery soup. I sipped it tentatively – it was far too hot so I stirred it for a while with a nearby spoon.

"A potion, Mum. I'm not going into details just yet. It's still top secret!" I replied. I rarely told my parents about my inventions. I know my dad had the same scientific ability as myself, and my mum had her own special ability (to turn invisible), but I still liked to work on my own creations in private.

"You *always* say it's top secret, Polly. What did you do with your last top secret creation? Those floating running shoes or whatever it was you were skidding around in?"

Mum was now mopping up the last of her soup with another soft chunk of bread. She was wearing a summery, flowery dress today with her hair up in a ponytail. She looked stunning to me, as always. I was still wearing my long white lab coat I wore when doing my experiments, and under this, my usual attire of jeans and checked shirt. I had gone for a slight change from the norm however and chosen a green shirt rather than the usual red or blue.

"My hover shoes were a gift for Betty. This potion I'm working on is a little something for Stefan," I said, and before Mum could quiz me further, I added, "That's all I'm saying about it."

At that moment, there was a knock at the door. It was a familiar, timid knock. Four quick, quiet knocks, a pause, and then four more knocks. I knew who it was before my dad got up and answered the door.

"Come in, Jamie!" I heard Dad say cheerfully as he opened the front door. "And you too, Ted! I know you're hiding under the window again!" Dad chuckled at this.

Ted and Jamie were now inseparable and had become the closest of friends. When not playing with me or Stefan or the twins, they were constantly scheming together in planning ever more elaborate scares for Jamie's dad.

"Hey, Pol!" Jamie exclaimed enthusiastically as he waltzed into the kitchen energetically.

"Hi Polly," Ted said as he followed Jamie and hid under the kitchen table.

I had just about got used to the unusual way in which Ted's voice seemed to enter into my head without passing through my ears first, like an unasked for thought. Ted, as usual, was dressed in rags. Jamie and his dad had tried to dress him up a little more smartly, but whatever he wore seemed to turn grey and tattered within minutes.

"How's it going guys?" I asked cheerfully. "Any more soup, Mum?" I added.

"There's plenty for everyone. You know me, Pol. I always make a giant pan full!" Mum replied and quickly offered two more steaming bowls onto the table for my friends. Jamie somehow managed to wolf his down in record speed, despite the fact it had just come out of a boiling hot pan. Ted crawled out from under the table and sipped his soup slowly.

"What's the latest invention, Polly?" Jamie asked as he watched Ted slowly finish off his soup. "You wouldn't tell us yesterday, you said you wanted a bit more time to work on it."

I didn't want to tell Jamie about my latest potion yesterday because I wanted to keep it as a surprise for him as well as for Stefan. That had been yesterday however, and that had been before I started having problems with my potion and getting frustrated with it. I decided that I would let Jamie help me with my creation. He had helped me in all of my other creations and they had all come out working brilliantly, so maybe I needed his help more than I first thought.

"It's a potion, I'll tell you more down in the cellar, come on!"

Before I could get up, I noticed my dad glaring at me from across the table. "I thought you were having a rest from the lab, Pol."

I glared back at my dad playfully. "I think the soup rejuvenated me, Daddy. I just wanna show Jamie what I have done anyway. I'll only be an hour or so."

My dad consented for me to leave with a wave of his hand and returned to the newspaper he was reading (a local weekly edition called the Wolfwich Chronicle that I noticed was delivered to our door every Tuesday – today was Wednesday). I ran down to the cellar, followed swiftly by Jamie and then Ted.

My potion was bubbling away in a huge pan, even larger than Mum's soup pan, on a small portable stove next to the vast stone table on which I had laid out all the ingredients I knew I needed. The three of us gathered around the pan like a trio of witches and looked at the potion. It was a bright blue, and every few seconds or so, a large bubble would erupt through the thick looking surface.

"What is it? Is it ready to try?" Jamie asked in a whisper, as though his voice might alter the potion in some way.

"I've not quite perfected it yet. There is one final ingredient I can't get quite right."

Jamie and Ted both looked at me as though I had just told them a circle had four sides. They were both used to me creating things effortlessly and without any fuss or problems.

"Yeah, I know," I sighed. "It's not like me, but I can't quite get the final measurement right. I know I need to add DNA extract, but I just can't recall how much I need."

"I thought it all just comes to you, like a brain explosion or something," Ted said.

"It does usually, Ted. It did do that yesterday when I started the potion, but now I just can't remember the final measurement."

We stared gloomily at the blue liquid for about a minute in silence and then Jamie's face lit up suddenly.

"When I forget where I leave my pencil case or something for school, Dad always tells me to close my eyes and concentrate on the item really hard and it's location generally pops into my head!" Jamie exclaimed.

It was a simple idea, but worth a try.

"Okay, guys, don't make a sound!"

I closed my eyes and pictured the last ingredient I needed. DNA extract was the most important ingredient of my potion – the key ingredient that would make the creature that drank it more human. Too little and there would be little to no affect. Too much and, well, I didn't want to find out what would happen if I gave too strong a dose in that situation! The powder was green and very fine and I had a kilogram of it in a jar on the table. I pictured the jar very clearly in my head. I knew a kilogram was far too much and that is why there was a teaspoon next to the jar. I pictured this spoon very clearly in my head also.

All I needed was half a spoonful to complete my potion ... I opened my eyes suddenly; it really was that simple – just half a spoonful!

"Thanks Jamie!" I said and kissed him on his pale green forehead. He blushed and I got to work instantly on finishing my potion. Without doubting that this was indeed the correct dosage – it was once again as clear as it had been yesterday – I measured off half a spoonful and tipped it confidently into the potion. Although nothing spectacular happened – it continued to bubble slowly and remained blue – I knew that the potion was now complete!

"*Now* it's done!" I declared proudly.

"What is it?" Jamie and Ted asked simultaneously.

"We need to find an animal," I said. "Any living creature that doesn't talk, and we will find out!"

ABOUT THE AUTHOR

Lee A. Smith is the author of Polly Peartree and the Great Wolfwich Mystery. When not working on upcoming sequels to Polly's adventures, and other stories, he enjoys watching old movies.

The Polly Peartree series:

Polly Peartree and the Great Wolfwich Mystery
Polly Peartree and the Vampire's Curse
Polly Peartree and the Time Travel Enigma